Fixing Perfect

Therese M. Travis

Fixing Perfect

COPYRIGHT 2014 by Therese M. Travis

Contact Information: titleadmin@pelicanbookgroup.com

All scripture quotations, unless otherwise indicated, are taken from the Holy Bible, New International Version(R), NIV(R), Copyright 1973, 1978, 1984 by Biblica, Inc.™ Used by permission of Zondervan. All rights reserved worldwide. www.zondervan.com

Cover Art by Nicola Martinez

Harbourlight Books, a division of Pelican Ventures, LLC
www.pelicanbookgroup.com PO Box 1738 *Aztec, NM * 87410

Harbourlight Books sail and mast logo is a trademark of Pelican Ventures, LLC

Publishing History
First Harbourlight Edition, 2015
Paperback Edition ISBN 978-1-61116-407-7
Electronic Edition ISBN 978-1-61116-406-0
Published in the United States of America

Dedication

To my grandchildren, those I know and those yet to come. And, as always, to my Heavenly Father, in everlasting gratitude.

Prologue

She was beautiful. He couldn't see another thing he wanted to fix. Her hair, her eyes, her posture—all of it perfect.

He reached forward to readjust a curl but stepped back without touching her. No. She was absolutely perfect. She filled some essential part of him with a joy so sharp it could cut his heart.

He completed his work as the sun came up, bathing the scene in a rosy, sun-risen glow. Just as he finished, he heard the thud and scrape of running shoes, far off, but coming closer.

He gathered his supplies and slipped away as the jogger reached the boundaries of the park.

1

The young woman's body told a thousand stories, offered up a thousand cryptic clues, and not the least were the wires, the padding, the propping. Her limbs stretched and posed like a dancer mid-plié, one graceful hand twisted and bent over her turned head. The worst was the glimpse her body gave into the warped mind of the monster who had killed her.

Sam Albrecht backed a little farther away, hiding his pulsating anger inside clenched fists. He had to wait to do his job, wait for the detectives to gather all those clues, wait for the photographer to take her pictures, wait for his rage to cool before he moved her.

The jogger who'd found her huddled far enough away that she couldn't see the corpse any longer. Not that hiding from the body would save her from seeing it behind her eyelids forever, or in her nightmares. Sam turned so as to be able to watch the woman as well as the crime scene, his muscles at ease but ready to jump to help her if she needed it. She held a paper bag in case she hyperventilated again, and her brown hair escaped her ponytail and clung to the sides of her damp face.

This far up from Avalon's harbor, nestled on the landward side of Catalina Island, the sound of the sea faded to background noise, like a hush of wind or the swish of tires on wet roads.

A car pulled up, not one of the few private

vehicles allowed on the island, but one bearing official plates, and another officer got out.

Detective Jerry Macias surveyed the scene for a short minute before he turned his massive body toward Sam.

"You OK, buddy?"

Sam narrowed his eyes, not meeting Jerry's gaze. The guy saw too much, understood too much, as it was. "Doing my job."

"Yeah. It smothers something inside you, doesn't it?" Macias nodded at the photographer and moved closer to the crime scene.

Sam went back to watching for the signal to load the body onto the gurney.

Seagulls wheeled overhead, curious, rapacious. Thank God the jogger found her before some of the more destructive animals got to her. At least her face hadn't been touched by ravening animals.

Only by the animal who had killed her.

Turn off the anger. Turn off the compassion. Turn off the gratitude that he wasn't the one who had to tell her family. Even more harrowing than seeing the glimpse into the killer's mind was the thought of dealing with her family's grief. What if it were his sister? One of his friends? Robin came to mind, her black hair swirling around her shoulders as she swung a bat, her blue eyes glinting with pride when she connected with the baseball, and he shuddered. *Not Robin, please, God, not Robin. Don't let this happen to Robin.*

He wasn't sure how he knew this wasn't the last painted and posed body he would deal with.

He took a breath when Macias started talking to the team. "It's Lehanie Haro. Her husband will have to identify her."

Most of the response team had already given the woman her name. Even the jogger had called in to say she'd found Lehanie. Everyone on the island had heard about her when she went missing. Mostly they'd speculated on why she'd kidnapped the little girl she'd been babysitting. Now, they'd have to wonder what the guy who had taken them both was planning to do to Becca. Five years old, and in a pervert's hands. Because a guy who could do this could do anything.

God, why do You let these things happen?

Sam glanced at the jogger, saw she held up for now, and looked back at the body.

Lehanie had flaming red hair. But now, it was a dull black, flat and dry. Sam wondered if the killer had made her dye it herself, or if he'd done it to her. He swallowed. The guy had tried to change the color of her eyes, as well, but at least all he'd done was paint blue irises on her eyelids.

The things he might be doing to the five-year-old made Sam wish he didn't possess much of an imagination.

Macias must have been thinking the same. "The little kid she was babysitting was blonde, right?"

"She *is* blonde." Sam wouldn't kill Becca off with his words before he had to.

"Yeah." Macias shrugged, obviously concentrating on only the immediate aspect of the case. "Rigor hasn't set in. The lady who found her OK?"

"Somewhat." Sam wasn't going to lie, no matter how expected. He peered at the wires wound through the woman's hair. He'd seen the telltale color at her roots, behind her ear. Her killer had posed her like a dancer and painted her like a stage performer.

He'd seen murders before, witnessed one himself not so long ago. But none of them sent his gut into cramps like this.

Sam's coworker, Trevor Graham, gripped Sam's shoulder. "Gotta move it. The photographer needs pics from this angle."

As he backed away, he once again had to turn off the emotions, the ache for the girl, her family, the small island community. But mostly, the fear for the little girl who, he had to believe, for now, was still alive.

৵৵ঌ

Robin Ingram pushed away from the counter and rolled her office chair to the cabinet where she stored her things. Hearing her name, she looked up at the man standing across the counter from her.

Hair bleached white blonde, skin a deep yet creamy tan, and eyes so pale a blue they looked like ice cube shadows, made up the stunning man's face. She'd seen him around town. The island didn't have a wide range of residents, so she knew most of the regulars by sight, at least. But she'd never talked to him. She wasn't even sure she knew his name.

"You are Robin, aren't you?" He slid papers onto the overflowing co-op counter and leaned his elbows on a woven tapestry a customer had spread out.

She blinked. "Yeah, that's me. But my shift is over. Sorry. Grace will be here in a minute, and she can help you."

"That's OK." He grinned. White teeth, dimples, the guy had it all, so dazzling he made Robin's eyes prickle. Made her kind of glad she'd never run into him face to face before. He could overwhelm any girl.

"Missy said to get this to you, and you'd process it in the next few days."

"Sure. No problem." She took the papers, scooted back to the file cabinet and laid them in the overflowing box atop it. She could have, but managed to resist, checking out the name on them. She'd do that later.

He smiled but didn't move.

His regard made her want to squirm. She raised one eyebrow. "Anything else I can do for you?"

"No." His slight frown cleared. "You have the most amazing eyes."

"Thank you." She straightened the stack in the inbox and scooted a little closer to the cupboard.

"Yeah. Beautiful baby blues. I'd love to photograph you." He laughed. "That's why I'm applying here. Get some of my photos out there, you know?"

"Oh, sure, this is a great place to sell your work." She grinned and slid her chair another half inch farther from the counter.

"Yeah." He waggled his eyebrows, more like he needed to acknowledge her wariness, than that he wanted to pull something over on her. "I've seen you around town."

He had to have.

"Avalon's a small place. You get to know the townies pretty quick. Have you been here long?"

"A couple months. I noticed you right off." He shifted his elbow and slid the tapestry closer to the edge.

Robin reached for it. "Sorry, this is merchandise. I need to put it back where it belongs."

"Oh, I can do that for you." He slung the

needlepoint off the counter and turned. "Where does it go? Oh, wait. I see an empty hanger over there." He crossed the store in a few long strides and clipped the fabric to the tiny clothespins on the hanger.

"Thanks."

"Sure thing. I'm happy to help." Again, he stared into her eyes for a little longer than comfortable. "It's really nice to finally get to talk to you."

Robin let herself relax. He was tall and good-looking, and he must have seen her try to walk, and here he was, still trying to flirt.

"Well, I've got to get back to work. You take care now." He raised one hand, strong and neat, and saluted her before he left the shop.

"Yeah, you, too." She didn't even know if he heard her. He didn't turn. Fair enough. She didn't quite know what to think of him. Looked like a celebrity and talked like a politician but he was probably harmless. Maybe even slightly interested.

She shook her head. If he'd seen her crutches, he couldn't be interested. He wanted photo subjects, not a girlfriend.

Robin didn't want a boyfriend, anyway. At least, not one who wasn't named Sam and didn't meet her for lunch every day she worked a shift at the co-op. She took a deep breath. Just because certain guys weren't attracted to her didn't mean no one would ever be. Didn't mean she'd turn off everyone just because she had a little disability. Didn't mean she'd ever want one of those accommodating, faceless men who'd settle for someone like her, either. But that disability meant if she didn't get moving right then she'd miss seeing Sam for lunch.

She waited for the door leading from the co-op

shop out to the boardwalk ringing the bay to close, checked out the guy's name on his paperwork, grabbed her backpack and crutches and heaved herself out of her rolling chair.

❧❧

A chilly wind danced its way from the beach, up the rocky and winding streets, and stopped to visit at the sole occupied bench in the tiny park before traveling on.

Sam breathed in the faint scent of brine and boat oil. Robin was late but she'd come. He wouldn't worry yet. Some days the trip from the shop to the park took her a little longer, though she usually managed a good clip.

And there she was, homemade backpack over her shoulders, painted denim jacket flapping with each swing of her crutches, and a hand-knit cap that matched her Pacific-under-a-brilliant-sun eyes. She looked up and something in those eyes caught at his heart. Those eyes had been doing that a lot, lately, and he wasn't sure how he felt about it. Sometimes he wanted to explore the message he found there; most times he shied away from how she made him feel, made him question. Although why he should question forming more of a relationship, he didn't know. Nothing wrong with one. He blinked, shoving that thought away for the moment.

When Robin eased onto the bench, she used one crutch for an extra balance point. He watched, but didn't reach out to help. Only if she started to fall would he offer. Better not to offend her. He'd done that once and didn't want to brave her wrath again.

Although her spirit made him grin.

Once settled, she shrugged out of the backpack and dropped it between them. "Sandwiches." She sounded a tad more breathless than usual, but one look at her face convinced him that was another subject he'd better not bring up.

He held out a brown paper bag. "Sodas." Italian cherry cream, kind of expensive but Robin's favorite. He liked to treat her once in a while. Or more often than that. And that made him uncomfortable, as well. But it didn't stop him from doing it.

"Perfect." She unfastened the pack and handed him a paper towel and a plastic-wrapped sandwich. It would be an entire meal, taste like ambrosia, and she wouldn't give him a list of ingredients even if he begged.

"If I tell you, you'll be able to make your own and then who will I have to eat lunch with?" she'd ask.

He always thought she was joking. "I'm too lazy to make my own lunch," he'd answer, but that never changed anything. Not that he minded. He just liked teasing her about it. Now, he said, "I'll say grace, OK?"

"Sure." She folded her hands and bowed her head, waiting for him to finish. She always said the same little poem she'd learned as a child, but he liked to put more variety into his thanks, sort of the way she treated her food creations.

"God of infinity, we thank You for our food, for the brilliant, talented hands that make it every day, for the beautiful weather, and for friendship. Be with us, guide us, and bless us as we finish our day." He almost added something about Lehanie Haro but stopped himself.

God knew about her death, may have already

welcomed her to heaven, but Robin might not have heard. He didn't want to add shock value to his prayers.

"Amen." She unwrapped her food, but slowly, as though she had more on her mind than eating. Maybe the news had reached the co-op.

He hadn't listened to the latest broadcasts.

Leaves spun down and littered the cracked cement walkway. Robin bent and swept a few together with one foot, but the breeze scattered them. She laughed and brushed several more out of her hair.

"You gonna eat?" He took a huge bite. She'd made his favorite, chicken salad with a yummy avocado dressing. He smiled around chewing. She liked to treat him just as often as he liked to treat her.

Sometimes he really liked what he thought that meant. Sometimes it scared him. Most of the time, he tried to ignore the questions that bubbled in his heart any time he thought of her. He wished they'd go away, but the thought of not seeing her, which was the only way he could think of to eradicate those questions, made his stomach hurt. So he just put up with the thoughts when he had to.

"Oh yeah." She took a much smaller bite, before she put the food back on the wrapper while she unscrewed the soda bottle. After that, she looked straight into his eyes, like she could read every thought he had. "Everything all right?"

He sighed. "You're going to hear about this soon enough. I thought you might have already. A jogger found the missing babysitter."

Despair filled her face. "Not Becca?"

He shook his head and knew before she opened her mouth that she understood the implication. "So

Lehanie is dead." Robin's lips pinched on the pain. "And she wasn't...she didn't have anything to do with kidnapping little Becca, did she?"

"She can't have. If she'd just turned up dead, the police might have still suspected her, but the way she was killed..." Murder and food did not mix. When was he going to learn that? He put down his sandwich.

Robin bent her head, her fingers worrying the beaded fringe of the scarf that peeked out from under the jacket. "So what does it mean?"

"It means there's someone really sick out there who still has a little girl." He remembered the way Becca looked in her pictures—soft, wispy blond curls, wide brown eyes, dimples on either side of her round chin. The pictures were everywhere, on posters and taped to plastic jars begging for donations, on the news and in the papers.

"She's so little." Her jaw clenched, biting off the words. "Just a baby."

"Yeah. I can't tell you any more details until I know for sure what the police will release to the media."

She nodded. "Does her family know?" She stumbled over her words. "Both families. They'll all have to hear. I can't imagine how Becca's parents will feel."

"By now, probably everyone has been told, yes. We got her out of there a couple hours ago." He finally managed to swallow bread sucked dry by sorrow. "Look, let's talk about something else, or we won't be able to eat."

She nodded again, her eyes distant and shadowed. "I hope you don't have nightmares."

So much for changing the subject. "I'll be all right.

It's been months."

"I know, but when I first saw you just now I thought—" She didn't tell him what was on her mind, didn't really have to.

The first few months after Henry's death, his murder had been all Sam talked about to her—the murder, the nightmares, his fears. And she'd listened. Over and over, to the same—or what probably sounded the same to her—details and guilt. And now he hadn't mentioned Henry or guns or dreams in a couple months. No wonder she worried.

"I'll be OK. It was ugly, really ugly, but I've seen stuff like it before." Not exactly like it, not even close. But he couldn't tell her that yet. "I'll be OK," he repeated.

"If you say so." Her wide blue eyes fastened on him, full of doubt.

"I do." He nudged her sandwich. "Come on, finish eating. I've got to walk you home pretty soon, and then get to bed. Two AM comes a little too early these days."

Her smile wavered and then strengthened. Good. Like all the other locals would be, she had to be devastated over Lehanie's death, but he didn't want it to bring her down. Didn't she have enough to worry about?

2

Late Friday afternoon Robin again sat behind the co-op gift shop counter, swinging one foot while she watched a few customers wander through the store. She tried hard to be glad any time anything sold, but she couldn't help the little thrill when it was something she'd made that someone picked up and, after deliberation, brought to the sales counter. The profit was nice; the satisfaction of having created something joyful was priceless.

Today, that thrill would be hard to come by, though not for lack of sales.

The store was made to entice women and children. Toys, hand-dyed blouses, hand-stitched purses, painted wood, and beaded ornaments crowded the shelves. A display of orange and purple Halloween items filled the narrow walkway leading from the front door to the belly of the shop, just begging kids to pop in and explore the offerings.

A couple with three little girls strolled inside.

Robin smiled at the woman and grinned outright when the oldest child went straight to the display of brightly dressed mermaids. She'd been making those dolls for more than a year, tweaking the design each time she put one together, and they were always a big seller.

"I've got matching paper dolls, too, right beside those."

The two older girls squealed while the youngest hugged a mermaid with a pink and orange tail.

The man stepped farther into the shop, glancing at the items for sale, but the mother hovered near the girls. When she saw Robin watching, she grimaced. "We just heard about that poor little girl and her babysitter. I mean, how they didn't find the little one." Her fist clenched over the youngest child's arm. "I'm not letting any of mine more than a foot away from me."

"I don't blame you." Robin half rose from the stool, but settled back down. "It doesn't make for a very relaxing vacation, though, I'll bet."

"It sure doesn't. You get so scared that some monster's gonna nab your baby. And don't even ask me about getting a babysitter."

The way the woman growled the words sent chills along Robin's neck. She didn't have kids, but she understood the fear.

The woman moved a step closer and lowered her voice. "They were locals, though, weren't they?"

Robin opened her mouth, at first resenting this woman's implication. But understanding took over. If those were her three little girls, wouldn't she grasp any hint of hope, no matter how small or how much it might hurt someone else, that they'd be just a little bit safer, because they didn't live on the island?

"They were. They are, I mean." She couldn't consign Becca to death without hope putting up a frantic fight, even if it was only over words. She rang up the family's sales and gave them a huge smile. "Stay safe."

"You bet."

A customer she'd been only marginally aware of

before wandered closer and leaned on the counter. She looked up into clear, pale blue eyes and started. Not a customer, then, but the photographer. She remembered the name from his paperwork. "Donovan, right?"

"You got it. You always here?"

"Me? No. Everyone does their share. I'm only here two days a week for three hours. If you get your photographs in, you'll have to do your time, too."

He grinned and nodded toward her display of dolls. "Those are yours?"

"The mermaids are, yes."

"They're cute. No wonder those kids couldn't leave without them."

"Oh, did you see that? The littlest one was so sweet." She let out a tiny breath.

He turned to stare out the door, his upper lip curling. "The mom was a little paranoid, though."

"I don't think so. She's a mother—and anyway, no one wants any little girls getting hurt. Much less what that—that *thing* did to the babysitter." She shuddered, remembering the few details Sam had been able to tell her. And even without specifics, dead was dead. No one wanted murder and kidnapping on the island. Lehanie had just gotten married and was probably planning her own family. "And who knows what he's doing to Becca."

He glanced at her, his eyes wide, at first, and then narrowed. "Right, yeah. Because she's still missing. I hadn't thought of that." Donovan scratched the back of his head. "But the way she acted, like they'd get snatched here in the store or even just because they're on the island. Overprotective."

Robin pinched her lips together. This guy just didn't get it. "But she might save her children's lives, and that's all that matters."

Donovan frowned. "But I was here. She saw me. It's not like I'd let anything happen to her kids and not do something."

She held out her hands. "People worry. It's not logical all the time."

"I getcha." He glanced around and leaned closer. "This is a really nice place. Did you give all my stuff to Missy yet?"

"Last night. She said she'd get back to you sometime today." She smiled, enjoying his movie-star perfection looks. "I really don't think it's going to be a problem. She's always looking for new talent."

"Great, thanks." He winked at her and strolled out.

She turned to the next customer, glad enough to make another sale, even if it wasn't one of her creations. But her heart was full of thoughts of Becca—five years old and who knew where.

❧

Alan Bricker stopped on the other side of the table from Sam, slapping his food onto the laminate as if it were responsible for the sickness of the murder. He yanked a leg over the bench and plopped down, running one hand over his haggard face, trying to disguise his horror with a show of bonhomie. "Sammy, boy, how you doing?"

"I'm all right. You?" Sam studied his friend. The older man, going gray and often complaining about the grim nature of police work, had become Sam's mentor the day he'd started working for the tiny Catalina Island ambulance service. He wasn't a paramedic, but he'd seen something in Sam that needed a father figure.

Bricker shrugged. "They put me on the dead girl's case. I like Macias, but..."

"Should I congratulate you or sympathize?"

Because it would be a great coup for the detective if he helped to solve it but a tremendous emotional drain, whether he did or not.

Bricker shook his head. "Who can tell? It's not gonna be good, no matter what happens." Again, he rubbed his face and stomach before glaring at the food. "I gotta get an easier job, but first I've got to take care of this pervert. You were one of the first responders, weren't you?"

Blinking at the change of subject, Sam said, "Yeah."

"What did you notice? Anything odd?"

"What? Like the fact that the killer dyed her hair? Painted eyes a different color from hers on her eyelids? Or the fact that he'd posed her and tied her down to keep her that way—like he thought she could still move?"

"Eh." Bricker leaned over his meal. "You saw all that?"

"Kind of hard to miss."

"We're dealing with a real sicko."

"I think the whole town knows that."

"Except the sicko."

"Yeah, maybe he hasn't figured it out yet." Sam dug into his burrito. "What creeps me out the most is the way he dyed her hair. What was the point? She wasn't pretty enough the way God made her?"

"Who knows why these guys do what they do? It's not our job to analyze him, just catch him. Heck, it's not even your job. You just get to transport the bodies."

Sam shook his head. Lehanie's hair still bothered him. Thick, dead black, and straightened. In her pictures, he'd always noticed Lehanie's bright red curls first.

అఒఇ

They didn't get it. They were all average. They had to be not to understand—not the message, not the beauty, nothing. His artistry was brilliant, beyond the scope of the average mind. Of course, he'd expected some resistance at first, expected a few people to fight his unique use of art materials. Wasn't that a sign of artistic genius—that most of the world didn't understand him or his art? No one appreciated the living artist.

But these people—they complained. They cried. They didn't *see*.

He'd just have to do his best to make them see.

అఒఇ

Saturday morning at the park meant the city bus dropping off team members, mostly children, young people confined to wheelchairs, or chained to crutches, like Robin, trapped in bodies that didn't conform or minds that didn't measure up to a lot of society's strict standards. It meant a chance for a lot of people to do their best, show their stuff, and be just like everyone else.

It meant Extreme Baseball.

Robin shrugged her bag over her shoulder and checked her laces one last time. The week before one had gone loose and tripped her. Today, she'd double knotted them, just like a kindergartener. But she'd long given up cringing at what she had to do in order to live a full life. Once she was sure her shoes wouldn't betray her, she shuffled to the front of the bus and let the driver hand her off the lift.

"Perfect day for a game, isn't it?" He stuck a wad of gum into his mouth and walked beside her. "Does me some good to watch you guys play."

"Why's that?" Robin paused to pull her hair off her face.

"No competition. Everyone cheers everyone else on. Gives a real definition to the word community, you know?" He glanced at her, his eyes slitted. "Something we all need to remember right now."

She nodded. The tension since Lehanie's murder had ratcheted up exponentially the last week.

Kerry, a developmentally delayed teen, lumbered up next to them. His bright white uniform hung on his scrawny frame, and his eyes vied with the sky for brilliance. One arm and hand curled into his side and the same-side leg was shorter than the other, setting his walk a little jagged, as if he were off balance. "Hey, Robin, I get to bat first today. Coach Danny says so. He says I earned it. He says—he says—yeah. He says I get to bat first."

"That's awesome. No waiting." Robin let one crutch fall against her hip so she could give Kerry a high five. He returned it with his good hand.

"Yeah, no waiting. It's awesome." He turned to the coach. "It's awesome, Coach Danny. I get to bat first. It's awesome."

The coach ruffled Kerry's hair and sent the young man to practice a few swings before he turned to

Robin. "I haven't seen your runner yet."

"He'll be here. He called this morning and said he might be a few minutes late. He had a meeting at work."

Danny nodded. "I'll put you a ways down on the hit list so it gives him time."

"That's fine with me. I don't mind waiting. Maybe you should just put me last." She glanced at Kerry, who had dropped the bat and was shouting his up-first news to another arrival. "I love that guy, you know?"

"He's one of the best." Danny tucked his clipboard under his arm and put his whistle to his lips. The shrill summons gathered enough of the team around him that the others noticed. The din faded, and he handed out assignments. Kerry and his runner, a teenager with wrestler's muscles and football cleats, named Aaron, got into position.

Danny strode to the pitcher's mound. "Batter up?"

"I'm here! I get to bat first!" Kerry gripped the bat close to his ear with his one good arm, and Aaron's help. He crouched, waiting for the pitch. It came slow. Kerry swung and missed.

"Not bad, Kerry." Robin called from behind the fence. "Keep swinging, you're gonna get a hit soon." She let go of one crutch and leaned hard into the chain link, letting it bounce her gently while she shouted encouragement.

He finally connected on his seventh pitch. His runner helped him drop the bat to the dirt and ambled next to him as Kerry shuffled to first base. Only when he reached the base, high fived the baseman, and got a drink from the bottle his runner held out, did the next batter grab a bat and hunch over home base.

Robin scanned the park. No Sam. Danny would

make sure she had someone else for a runner if she needed one, but she was more worried about Sam than her place in the game. He'd sounded so down on the phone, and the meeting was about Lehanie. The case had him wound as tight as his old partner's murder always did, and she couldn't fix it for him. Yet. She'd get him to talk eventually, but he was resisting. The sooner she did, the better.

Her gaze meandered from the lineup across the park. The usual number of families dotted the grass and the playground was almost as full as any other Saturday. Robin noticed more adults, and an atmosphere of heavy vigilance. They'd keep the kids safe, keep each other safe. If they could.

Donovan stood, feet planted wide, a few yards beyond third base. A camera hung around his neck, and he grinned as the second batter swung and connected. He joined in the cheers, caught Robin's eye, and wound his way through parents and siblings to her side.

"Robin, how you doing?" He followed the runners with his camera. His shutter clicked every half second as he captured the play.

"Just ducky. You taking pictures to sell at the co-op?"

"Not of this game."

She turned away, her jaw clenched. Maybe the players weren't the showcase of cuteness, but they were people, deserving of dignity, and why was he standing here watching, taking shots, if he didn't think they were worth his time?

"Gotta get all kinds of parental permissions and stuff. But I thought I'd offer to do team pictures. Then, I can make sure people know I'm OK to hang around, and no one will mind." He nodded to where Kerry had just trundled across second base. "He's a cute kid. He's got something special."

"He does, but he's not a kid. He's almost twenty."

"Really? He's pretty small."

"Comes with the territory. A lot of the team have growth issues in one way or another."

"Yeah?" He looked over the field, his right hand stroking the camera. "You play? I mean, do you get out there on the field and bat and everything?"

She shifted one crutch to angle her body away from him. "Of course. Why else would I be wearing a uniform?"

His gaze roved her white shirt and pants. "OK. You got a runner like everyone else?"

"Yup. Regulation rules and all."

"Who is it?" He lifted the camera to his eyes again and adjusted the focus.

"A friend of mine." Though why she was so unwilling to share Sam's name, she couldn't explain, not even to herself.

"Yeah? Where is she?"

Robin lifted her chin. "Not here yet. It's OK, though, if he doesn't get here in time, Danny'll find someone else for me. No one ever loses a turn because of a runner not showing up."

Donovan's eyes lit up. "I'll be your runner."

"Mmm, I don't know. Danny likes to use people he's already cleared, you know? Especially these days."

"Oh, yeah, I see that. Can't be too careful. I just figured since you're not a kid it would be all right."

"It would be, if it weren't for the actual kids. I've got to set a good example, you know."

"Right. Got it." Again, Donovan looked over the field. He lifted his camera again, using it like a pair of binoculars. "This is a great game. I don't know why I've never run across it before. You guys meet every Saturday morning?"

"Yup."

She leaned against the chain link again and gathered her hair in one fist. Strands whipped across her face, so she let go of the whole lot and started over.

Donovan turned, his eyes narrowed against the wind. "Hey, want me to help you with that?"

"No, it's OK. It won't take me but a minute."

"It's OK. I can fix you right up."

Robin wrapped the hair band around the ponytail, tightened it with a few twists and gave him a wide smile that probably showed too many teeth. "All done. No problem. I have bad legs, not hands."

He blinked. "Oh, that's not what I meant."

"I know." Even though she didn't. But manners dictated she relieve his embarrassment. "Everything's fine."

"Yeah, but if you ever want me to fix something for you, just let me know."

"Sure thing." He was trying hard, at least, which was better than some people she'd run into.

"I'm really good at fixing things. You should—"

Behind her, Sam said, "Where are you in the line-up?"

Robin turned, grinning. "Dead last."

Sam twinkled back. "Good. Who got to go first?"

"Kerry."

"Oh, boy, I bet he was excited." Sam bent to straighten the cuff of his jeans. "I kind of rushed over. I think I remembered to put on all my clothes."

Robin laughed. "If anything's missing, someone will let you know."

"Probably Kerry." He straightened and looked over at Donovan.

"I wouldn't doubt it."

She studied his face as he watched the other man. No sign of jealousy. She sighed. Why had she even pretended she could expect him to care if another man talked to her? "Sam, do you know Donovan? He's a photographer. He just joined the craft co-op."

Sam lifted his chin in greeting, though he waited a moment before saying anything. "Welcome. Are you part of the team or—?" He let his tone finish the question.

"No, just came across it. I only met Robin a few days ago. Pretty cool to run into her twice." He winked at her.

Well, let Sam see that other men were interested. Then she remembered, and told Donovan, "Sam is my runner."

"I figured." He shifted the camera to the other side of his chest. "I'm going to see if I can get a better vantage from across the field. See you around." He strode off.

After a moment, Sam said, "Nice guy."

"You didn't take to him, either." Though why she felt the need to defend Donovan, she had no idea. It wasn't like Sam cared.

"Hey, I said he was a nice guy."

Robin snorted.

Kerry jostled Robin's elbow. "Hey, Robin, you're up. Come on! It's your turn. Hurry up!"

Sam wrapped his arm around her shoulders to keep her from tipping over under Kerry's enthusiasm.

He followed her to home base, fetched her preferred bat, and stood behind her, the bat in his outstretched hand in front of her.

Robin slipped her arms from the crutches, leaned back against Sam's chest, and gripped the wood in both hands. Sam tucked the crutches against his hips. After he brushed her hair from her neck, he tucked his head against her back.

Sam said, "Ready." His arms went around her waist.

She could stay this way forever. Sam's forearms crossed over her stomach and his palms pressed against her ribs, the way Danny had taught him. Her crutches nestled in the crook of his elbows, so they wouldn't fall, and neither would she.

"Ready!" Robin called to the coach.

"Batter up!" Danny wound and let fly a faster ball than his usual. Robin swung, but the ball continued to the catcher's mitt.

"Steady up." Sam shifted against her back, and she felt his breath warm on her shoulder blades.

How was she supposed to concentrate on a bit of rawhide and thread when she had Sam breathing deliciously down her neck? Ah, but she had to. This was not the place to lose her mind, as attractive as it seemed. She choked the bat again and called, "Ready."

Danny pitched.

This time her swing caught the ball dead on, and it flew to the outfield. Robin squealed, dropped the bat and reached back with both hands.

Sam fitted the crutches over her wrists and waited for her to get her balance before he stepped back.

Robin had never mastered running, but she could hustle well enough. Her pace gave her time to watch as the outfielders tossed her ball to each other, stalling until she reached first base.

Sam jogged beside her, more to give her the impression of speed than because he had to, to keep up. "That was a great hit. You've got some good arm muscles going there."

"Comes from having to use them to walk. You want to build up your pecs, I recommend crutches. Of course, your legs get kind of wimpy after a while."

He laughed as she touched first base. "There's nothing wimpy about you."

Well, her heart might argue that. It still wanted his arms around her, no matter the reason. Then again, she didn't want support. She wanted more.

❧

Out on the field, Sam caught three grounders and pretended to fumble them while the players headed off for first base. Once they were started, he'd give an easy toss to someone else on the field. Eventually, when the player got to first base, someone would pass the ball to the pitcher's mound and let Danny stall. Sam let one fly ball land between him and Robin, making sure it wouldn't hit her on the head. He tossed her the ball and she sent it on to the outfield, watched it travel between teammates until the player made it across home base, to the cheers of "home run!"

When the game wound down Coach Danny gathered his team around him for a final thank you and prayer before they headed back to the bus. They'd go to the pizza parlor, and after lunch and video games, the bus driver would drop each player off in front of his or her home.

Sam and most of the other runners, as well as the players' families, followed on foot or in their golf carts. The parlor was three blocks from the field and as he walked, the photographer who'd been talking to Robin caught up with him.

He wished the guy would find something else to do. Go take pictures of stunning models or something, anything to get him away from watching Robin with that look in his eye.

Funny. He hadn't known he could be so jealous.

"You're Sam, right?"

As if Robin hadn't introduced them just an hour before. Donovan barely glanced at Sam as he marched next to him.

"That's me." Now he could leave. Sam wouldn't mind.

"Thought so. You're Robin's runner."

Sam nodded and glared at the coach's back. Something about this Donovan guy felt like saw grass inside his sneakers, but maybe it was the way he talked about Robin, as though she belonged to him simply because—what? He knew her? Because he wanted to sell his work through the same co-op she did?

"She's a beautiful young woman. I told her I wanted to take some photos of her, but it seemed to make her a little nervous. She doesn't seem all that shy, though."

Sam shrugged. "I don't know too many women who like having their pictures taken." His sister often hid her face or turned away when a camera lens pointed at her.

"You don't think it's because of her disability?"

Sam stopped walking, his hands clenched. "I think it's because she's a perfectly normal human being."

"Oh, yeah, of course she is. Well. More beautiful than most. Right?"

"Look, I know that, and you know that. But try convincing Robin—" But no, he didn't want this guy anywhere near Robin. "It's just normal," he finished, feeling he'd let his best friend down in his defense of her.

"What would be best," Donovan said, "is to fix everything for her. Her legs. So she can walk like anyone else. Run, play baseball the way she's meant to. Live a normal life. You know. Be perfect."

And if he said a word of that to Robin, she'd deck him. Sam hoped he was around to see it.

3

Robin helped Kerry maneuver onto the bench next to her and waved at his mother to let her know he was fine. The young man's hands shook with fatigue, but his face shone. "I was up first. I batted first today."

"You sure did." Robin edged onto the bench next to him. It took a while, since she was almost as tired as Kerry, but he kept talking the whole time.

"I made a homerun. I batted first and then I made a home run."

Robin grinned. "You did. I saw you. You did great."

"I did great. I was awesome." He pumped his good hand in a triumphant fist.

Robin wrapped her arm around his shoulder, partly from sheer affection, and partly to keep him from tumbling off the bench in his excitement. "You're always awesome, Kerry."

"I know. You, too." Kerry looked across the table and up a few seats. "Who's that camera guy? He kept doing his camera all the game." Kerry mimed focusing a camera and clicking the shutter repeatedly.

Robin glanced in the same direction.

Donovan curled around his camera which sat on the table in front of him, his arms forming protective walls encircling it. As if he were waiting for her to notice him, he looked up.

She nodded to him. "That's Donovan. He wants to

take pictures of the whole team."

"To put on the wall?"

"If you want to." And, of course, Kerry would want to.

"Or maybe in the newspaper. Sometimes they put pictures of teams in the newspapers."

"Maybe they'll do that." She pulled her hair band out and flipped her hair over her shoulder. Donovan had to be the best looking guy on the island, and maybe that was why Sam disliked him on sight.

Good. Maybe that would make Sam take a real look at her.

She gave Donovan a warm smile and focused all her attention on Kerry, who repeated everything he'd already told her at least three times before the pizzas arrived. Robin served him two huge slices of pepperoni, tucked a napkin under his chin, and made sure his soda was capped and the straw was pushed all the way to the bottom of the cup before she started on her own lunch. When Sam slid in next to her, she leaned against his shoulder for half a second and grinned at him. "I saved you a slice of veggie pizza."

"You never have to save it. None of the kids like it." He helped himself and took a huge bite.

She shifted a little so her legs weren't splayed out under the table. "Do you have to go back in to work today?"

Sam swallowed. "Not until tomorrow afternoon. This morning was a sort of debriefing. And they offered some counseling as well."

"That's good."

His jaw flexed before he said, "I told you. I don't need it. I'm fine. No nightmares last night."

Her heart ached at the pain in his voice, which he

wouldn't acknowledge. "And if you did, would you tell me?"

"Sure. I'd tell you. Don't I tell you everything?"

His low voice tickled her ear. She rubbed it and glanced up the table. One of the team moms sat next to Donovan, talking away and gesturing at his camera. Donovan turned away from watching Robin, and without the warmth in his eyes, she shivered.

"What's wrong?" Sam paused in the act of snagging another slice.

"Nothing, really. Just—I don't know. Lehanie and everything, I suppose."

Sam patted her shoulder absently before he turned back to his lunch. "Right. I don't blame you. Everyone's on edge." He bent to give her a searching look. "Maybe you're the one who needs to go in for the counseling."

"Why? I didn't even know her." Robin remembered the mother who had come into the shop with her three daughters. "But we *should* be on edge. We should be worried and sad and vigilant, looking for the guy. This isn't something we can ignore." The picture of Lehanie the news media ran constantly rose up behind her eyelids, the way it had been doing since Sam told her they'd found her body. Closing her eyes brought her picture up like a movie running in a continuous loop; opening them brought home the juxtaposition between the young woman's reality and wherever Robin happened to be at the time.

Sam gripped her hand. The warmth of his fingers helped.

Kerry clambered off the bench, bumping Robin. "Sorry, Robin." He swung his leg over, kicked her thigh. "Sorry. Sorry, Robin."

"It's OK." Robin shifted closer to Sam and grinned as Kerry grabbed Danny's sleeve. "I got to bat first, Coach. You let me bat first. It was awesome."

"Who taught him his new word?" Sam asked.

Robin bent close to him. "Me, I think. We keep telling each other we're awesome."

"Absolutely true." He lifted his head and his mouth pinched for half a second before he nodded at someone behind Robin. "Hey."

Robin turned to see Donovan had moved around the table and now stood next to her. She scooted away from Sam's shoulder, again smiling at Donovan.

"Hi. Mind if I sit here? I think the little guy isn't coming back for a while."

Sam's jaw dropped. "Do you mean Kerry?"

"Yeah. Sorry. I don't mean to belittle him. I'm having a hard time remembering he's older than he looks."

"Maybe you need to try harder." Sam's hard tone cracked across the space, and Donovan hesitated marginally before he climbed over the bench and reached across the table for the pitcher of soda.

"I will. I promise. I haven't spent much time with handicapped kids, but that doesn't mean I'm judging them."

Robin hoped she was the only one who heard Sam's grunt of disbelief.

Donovan's gaze shifted to her, slid across her, and back. "I was wondering. He keeps saying he hit a homerun, but I thought he stopped on first base."

"Right. But he made it home, and any run is a homerun in Kerry's vocabulary. Make that the whole team. Everyone hits a homer, even though nobody gets past first when they get their hit."

"OK, that makes sense. He obviously loves to play and loves to win. Except, neither team won. No one struck out, no one got tagged out, and every single player crossed home base."

Robin nodded. "Because it's about playing, not about winning. Extreme Baseball has a very different focus from any other team game in the world."

"I guess." Donovan took a long swallow. "It's kind of nice."

His tone made her like him even more.

Donovan set down his cup. "You do this every week?"

"As long as the weather's good, and on the island, that's pretty much every week. We might miss three games a year due to rain. That's about it. A few more last year, with all the storms."

"Right." Donovan nodded and stood. "I'm going to go have a chat with the coach, see if he wants to set up some shoots. Before the game would be great. I'm thinking of giving each player a free copy, standard photo size, or a five by seven, maybe, and then if people want more, well, I can work out a deal. What do you think?" He glanced down at Robin.

"I think that's very kind." And that he'd make a lot of money on it. Did he have any idea how self-serving he sounded? But then, he was a businessman, trying to get customers, like anyone else. And all her teammates would love having a picture of the whole team together.

Sam relaxed as soon as Donovan walked away. He wrapped his arm around her shoulder, and then let it slide to rest near her waist. "I hope he takes the picture next week and disappears."

❧❧

Becca snuggled next to Mr. Bird while he smoothed her hair and tucked a strand behind her ear. Her daddy used to do that to her, after her bath, and he also tickled her until she squealed and couldn't breathe for laughing. Then he'd read her a story before Mommy tucked her into bed and listened to her prayers.

Everything was different since Mommy and Daddy made Lehanie give her to Mr. Bird. Maybe it was because she never had to take a bath, or put on clean clothes, or go to school, or because she never got to go outside. She missed those things, even though when Mr. Bird told her she didn't have to do them, he made it sound like he was giving her a big old present.

She missed Mommy and Daddy a lot, though, and Mr. Bird never explained that as something good.

Now, she sat on the lumpy, skinny mattress, tipped toward Mr. Bird because his weight made a dip, and let him pet her. It made her feel closer to Daddy, like if she believed hard enough, he'd come instead and take her home.

"You were a very good girl today. What do you want for a reward? Ice cream? An extra cookie?"

"I want my mommy." She stared up at the big man. He was taller than her dad, and he didn't have a beard like her dad. He had light blond hair and blue eyes that made her feel cold sometimes. She snuffled and rubbed her nose with the back of her hand.

Mr. Bird handed her a tissue and wrapped his fingers over hers and helped her wipe. Her daddy did that, too. "I want my daddy. I want to go home."

"I know, baby." He folded the tissue over to hide

the snot and tossed it into the can pushed up to the wall. It bounced out, but that didn't matter, because the can was too full to hold anything else. Mr. Bird never emptied it. "And they'll be back pretty soon, I promise. But right now all I can give you is something sweet."

"Why couldn't you let Lehanie stay with me? She takes care of me when Mommy and Daddy are gone at work." She hunched her shoulders. "Sometimes I get scared."

"I know." He patted her shoulder. "See, Lehanie had to do a job for me. And she did great. She was beautiful." His eyes went funny, and he stroked her hair. "Beautiful black hair, she had."

"No, she didn't." Becca was being a grumbly old bear, and she knew she shouldn't, but Mr. Bird never cared, anyway. "She had red hair."

Now Mr. Bird looked right at her, and the funny look went from his eyes. "I fixed her."

Becca didn't understand how red hair had to be fixed. Her hair wasn't black, either, and Mr. Bird didn't mind. "Why do I have to stay here?"

"Oh, that's easy." Mr. Bird smiled. "You're going to help me, too. Not just yet. I have to get everything set up. Don't worry, though. I know exactly how you're going to help me. You look just like her."

Becca liked helping. "Daddy says I look just like Mommy."

"No. You look like my robin. Only she has black hair." Again, he stroked her hair.

Becca wondered if it turned black under his hand.

"But right now, I want to do something nice for you. What do you want? I have cookies and ice cream."

"My daddy likes to read me stories." She told him

about her daddy all the time, but he never remembered anything.

"I guess I can do that. Go brush your teeth and pick out a book. After that you've got to go right to bed."

She slid off the mattress and hurried to the bathroom. She had a little trouble with the cap on the toothpaste tube, but soon she finished her job and she hurried back.

Mr. Bird had turned off the extra flashlight.

"I don't like it dark." She climbed back onto the mattress and put her arms around her knees. It made her feel safer to curl into a ball. As soon as Mr. Bird left, there wouldn't be much light in the room at all, except for one yellow bulb right up in the ceiling, and it scared her.

"Did you pick out a book?"

"I forgot." She scooted off again and went to the tiny pile of books by the other wall. He held the flashlight so she could see a little. Not that she needed to see very well. There weren't many books, and she'd looked at all the pictures already, but she pulled out the one that made her think most of her dad. And Lehanie. Her babysitter used to read it to her, too, and ever since Mr. Bird took Lehanie away, Becca'd been pretty scared. Especially about going to sleep. She didn't like to go to sleep all by herself.

Wait. This time Mr. Bird didn't say Lehanie went back home. He said she did a job for him. But maybe Lehanie did the job and went home. Becca hoped she got to do her job soon. She wanted to go home so bad.

When she put *The Gingerbread Man* into Mr. Bird's hands, he smiled and lifted her onto his lap. Sometimes that made her feel funny. He wasn't her dad. He said he wasn't a stranger, but she couldn't remember him from when she was little, or from when she lived with her mommy and daddy. But he never did any of the things her mom said were very, very bad, like touching her where she went to the bathroom, so she let him hold her.

He gave her a little squeeze before he opened the book. "It'll be all right, Becca. I promise. You're going to be perfect."

She nodded and stared at the first page. The little gingerbread man was so cute. She never liked the end of the story, but she always pretended the fox didn't eat the cookie. Mr. Bird's voice, soft and musical, lulled her eyelids heavier and heavier, until he shut the book and turned to pull the sheet down. "OK, little bird. Time for bed." He laid her down and tucked the sheets up to her chin. "Sleep well."

"You, too."

He grinned and tapped the end of her nose with his finger. Then he and his flashlight were gone.

After he left, Becca put her thumb in her mouth and turned so she could reach between the mattress and the wall.

He probably wouldn't like the little hole she'd started to make in the paint. He'd probably look at her, his cheeks hanging like a sad puppy, his pale eyes sorry, and tell her how disappointed he was with her. And she didn't want to make him sad. Or mad. But she couldn't help herself. One thumb went into her mouth, and the pointer finger of her other hand dug at the hole, a little deeper, and a little deeper. Something flaked off under her fingernail. In the morning she'd have little bits of white stuck there, and she'd have to scrape them out with her teeth. But she couldn't get to sleep if she didn't dig. Just a little.

Some nights she had to dig harder to make the scary dreams go away.

After a minute, she sat up. She'd forgotten her prayers again. She flapped her hand in front of her face, the way her mommy taught her, and whispered, "Ina nama Father ana Son ana Holy Spir-t, Jesus, bless Mommy and Daddy and Mr. Bird. Help Mommy and Daddy come home fast. Help me do my job soon so I can go home. And help me be good. Help me not make a mess of the wall anymore. Amen." She made another Sign of the Cross and stuffed her hand under her bottom. In a short time, she found it had sneaked back to the forbidden place, over the edge of the mattress and back to the hole. It was bigger. She could fit two fingers in now.

Mr. Bird wouldn't like it. But her fingernail kept digging, and the tears kept trickling salt into her mouth.

തൈ∽ൈ

He stood outside the door and listened. No sound. Good. She was a good kid. She'd be useful. Not yet. Not for a while, but he had plans.

First, he had to make sure the world understood what he was saying. They hadn't gotten it last time. All that work with Lehanie, getting her ready, making sure no one found her before he was ready, making sure nothing disturbed his canvas, and they hadn't understood. There'd been a few of the right reactions. He had to give them that. But they'd missed the big message. They still didn't *see*. After all his work, after the black hair and blue eyes, they didn't get it. What would it take to get through to them?

He had a lot of work to do. He wanted to get started as soon as possible, but he had to be careful now.

He was good at careful. Good at telling his stories through his art.

4

By the time Robin clipped into the shop, Grace had finished restocking the co-op shelves. Robin maneuvered her crutches around a new pile of baskets, edged between a rack of quilted jackets and a second hand dresser whose drawers overflowed with handmade jewelry. She spent a minute checking out a few new items before she settled behind the counter.

"Any good sales today?"

Grace laughed. "Lots. And, my gosh, you wouldn't believe. That new guy, Donovan, the photographer? He came in and left some of his photos. You should check them out. I put three up behind the register."

Startled, Robin turned. "I didn't even notice we had anything new over here."

The photos were beautiful. One depicted Avalon Bay from on high. Sun poured from the south and heavy clouds threatened from the north. He'd angled the camera to get a glimpse of the California mainland on the horizon. The one in the middle showed a family of three, a mom and dad and a little girl wearing a soft, floating white shift, walking hand in hand across the beach, facing away from the camera. The wind blew their hair the same direction as their shadows. Even from the back Robin could tell the little girl was laughing. The third was a close up of some of the wildflowers indigenous to Catalina Island.

"Wow, he's good."

"Isn't he? And gorgeous besides." Grace leaned her elbows on the counter and stared at the pictures. "Too bad I'm too old for him."

"Not by much. But unfortunately, you're married."

"Oh, I don't know. A man that good-looking might tempt me."

Robin laughed. Grace adored her husband.

"But I'm not the one who's caught his fancy. You should have heard him asking about you. Wanted to know every detail I could come up with. I'm telling you, he likes you."

Robin parked one crutch against her hip and tried to manufacture the correct surprise. "Me?"

"Yup. Asked when you'd be in, how long you'd stay, how much money you made on each sale. He wanted to make sure I told you he bought some of your things. He's going to send them all the way to Michigan to his nieces. And that he was sorry he missed you. And how much he enjoyed the baseball game and the pizza afterward. Oh, and he had plenty of questions about Sam, too. Like, did I think Sam was a serious contender. He's very interested." Grace's eyes gleamed, and her cheeks bulged in a wicked smile. "You ought to snag him up in a hurry."

"Who says I'm interested in him?" Robin turned away, fighting the need to ask Grace what her answer to Donovan's last question had been. Was Sam serious? Or just a good friend? But then, Robin had a pretty accurate idea of Grace's opinion on Sam's intentions. She'd probably told Donovan that Robin was his by default and promised to plan the wedding if he needed help.

Grace slapped a hand on the counter. "Robin! He's gorgeous and talented. What's not to like?"

Robin stuffed her backpack into the space behind the counter. "I'm not saying he's not a catch. He's pretty gorgeous, just like you said. But there aren't any—there just aren't any sparks."

"Like there are every time you see Sam."

"Like that, yes." Robin couldn't help a quick look around the store to make sure no one who knew Sam was within hearing distance. Only a couple of middle-aged women had entered, and they were discussing a selection of scarves.

"Sam doesn't feel it, though. Honestly, Robin, when are you going to wake up to that? You're a great therapist, but not a lover. In his eyes, I mean."

Robin bent her head. How did Grace pick up on the one thing that worried Robin the most?

"Honey, you can't spend your whole life waiting for Sam to notice you're a woman. Here you've got someone who's fantastic and, besides that, interested." Grace paused in restocking earrings to give Robin a searching look. "Don't let him get away while you're waiting on Sam."

"Gee, thanks. You sound like my grandmother." Robin swung onto the stool and pushed at a few papers Grace had left on the counter. "You're taking your break now, aren't you?"

"I didn't mean to offend you—"

"Don't worry about it." Robin wouldn't. She'd crawl under her own little personal rock as soon as she got the chance and cry, maybe, but she wasn't going to worry. Because whatever Sam might think of her or feel about her, he was her best friend and always would be. If it never got any further than that, she'd have his friendship, and she refused to do anything to jeopardize what their relationship meant to her. Even if it meant never asking for more.

Even if it meant passing up her only chance.

"Robin." Grace turned her on the stool and put her hands on her shoulders. Her eyes gleamed with a hint of tears, and her forehead creased with concern. "Please don't be upset. You know I just want what's best for you. I want you to find love. And Donovan just might be the one."

"Why? Because he's the only one who's interested in a cripple?"

"I didn't say that—"

"No, of course you didn't. But you implied that I'd better snatch up the only adult, unattached male who shows the least interest in me, because if he finds someone else, the chances of someone as damaged as I am finding true love is nil."

"I didn't say that, either."

Robin turned away. She really had to get a grip on her tongue. She had no right talking to her friend that way. "Look, just go. Please? I'll handle the shop until you come back, and then I'm off. I'm not feeling too well today."

Grace's eyes crumpled. "You mean you're mad at me."

"Whatever. Sure. I'm mad, and I really don't want to be here today."

"All right." Grace collected her purse and headed for the door. She stopped on the threshold. "And for what it's worth, I'm sorry. I didn't mean to make you feel like you're—whatever you're feeling."

"Right."

Robin watched Grace walk out of the shop, her

shoulders hunched. What was wrong with her that she could treat her friend that way? She had no right.

After a glance at the two customers, Robin folded her hands and shut her eyes. *Oh, God, loving Father. First, forgive me. You don't want me to treat Grace that way, and I'm sorry I disappointed You.*

A peek told her she still had time to finish her prayer before she had to get to work.

Show me how I'm supposed to deal with people who seem to think I'm half worthless and no one wants me. Please. And—

Before she could go into her long list of complaints, not to mention all her intercessions, a clearing throat startled her eyes open.

The two women had made their choices and waited for her to ring them up. After that, the store got busier. One of the ferries must have recently dropped off a load from San Pedro.

As soon as Grace came back from her break, Robin packed up her backpack and headed out.

Grace called after her.

Robin turned back to let her friend give her a brief hug. "I shouldn't have talked to you that way. I'm sorry. But I really am tired," Robin said, and cringed at the excuse. She only hoped it would make up for her querulous behavior.

Still, the conversation left her clenching her fists tighter than normal on her crutches. Where did people get off assuming that because Robin's legs weren't perfect, no reasonable man would want her? Grace wasn't alone in her prejudice; most people seemed to assume that Robin was the one who had a twisted view of her own worth.

I am a child of God. He loves me, and because of Him, I

have worth.

Too bad she couldn't believe herself. Too bad she couldn't treat her friend as if Grace possessed that same belief.

God, I don't want to be like this. I want to love the way You do. Can I? Can You, through me?

She didn't want to go home too soon, or her grandmother might probe, and she was a woman who delved and dug until she'd ferreted out every conceivable secret. Robin never could decide if Gram's repeated questions were because of her insatiable need to get to every last detail or because her hearing aids didn't work as well as she claimed.

Since the whole issue of her worth wasn't one Robin wanted to share with anyone, she headed in the opposite direction, toward the classic styled, museum quality casino. She'd never make it to the building, not this week at least, not on foot, though she saw tourists straggling across the walkway to the entrance. But halfway across the curve that hugged the bay was a stone fountain with wide sides and a view of the water. She'd always liked to sit there and look at the boats in the marina and listen to the sounds of kids playing at the water's edge. They were a lot farther away, but their voices always carried.

There weren't many kids out today, though, probably because of the kidnapper—the murderer. Until Lehanie's body had turned up, there had been optimism that it wasn't one of those situations as well as lots of speculation that Lehanie had kidnapped Becca herself, but her murder had destroyed that hope.

The cold stone under Robin's jeans almost changed her mind about sitting there, but she ignored the discomfort and leaned her chin on the back of her hand, which in turn she rested on the top of one of her crutches.

Sailboats and yachts and every conceivable pleasure boat in between had berths. Many were covered with the bright blue, fadeless tarps, and sails were wrapped around masts. Donovan ought to take a picture here today.

But not of her. She thought of how he'd admired her eyes, and she shook her head.

She didn't dislike him. He was a nice guy, talented, and, as Grace kept pointing out, gorgeous. He looked like a model. He liked the kids on the team, didn't talk down to them when he could help it, and offered to do something nice for them. And he'd made it clear to both Robin and Grace that he liked her. Liked Robin. But she still wasn't interested, not like that. She couldn't make herself, any more than she could make Sam fall in love with her.

"Hey, beautiful. I thought you had to work this afternoon." Sam sprawled onto the stone beside her, seemingly oblivious to the cold.

"I left early." Robin shifted, trying to find a bit of warmth, but the fountain had leached all the heat from her bottom. "I was just thinking about heading home."

"Not feeling good?" Sam stood and waited while she hauled herself to her feet.

"Just mad." And now he'd ask why and what could she say?

"Who at? I hope you're not mad at me."

"Never." She grinned up into his handsome face. Maybe he didn't look like a model, but his face was more real, held a lot more honesty in it, and so was more attractive to Robin. She didn't want a man carved from marble, after all.

"OK, what's up? Come on, tell old Sammy."

Robin laughed, though it held a hint of the bitter anger she still felt. "Grace just said a few things that set me off, so after she came back from her break I ditched her. The shop isn't that busy this afternoon anyway. And I'll be there on Friday night."

"You're always there on Friday nights."

"Yup."

"She schedules you for date night because she figures you can't get a date?"

Robin sucked in a deep breath and mangled her crutches under her arms so she could heave herself to her feet. So humiliating to want to stomp away and have to take so much time over it.

Sam followed her easily. "That's it, isn't it? Grace said something to the effect that no guy is ever going to be interested in you, and you're mad."

She spun on the tip of one crutch, glaring at him, and he jumped. "What is it with you? How do you do that?"

His eyes went wary. "What? Put my foot in my mouth?"

"No. Read my mind."

"Is that what I was doing?" He drew level with her and looked at her sideways. His cautious expression would have made her laugh, and she'd have given into it if she weren't so close to tears. But she wouldn't cry in front of him. She'd stopped crying over her legs and their effect on her life years before. "Pretty much."

"Well, it's just common sense. Grace tends to be—a little tactless. Kind of like me, on occasion. And talking about date night—" He stopped, apparently realizing that subject was better left unexplored.

Therese M. Travis

"Anyway, yeah, I just figured it out."

"She thinks I should jump at the chance to go out with some guy I don't like—at least, not for a boyfriend—just because he's asked her a few things about me. She thinks if I don't, I'll waste my only chance at ever finding a guy willing to date a cripple."

"You've had other dates. In fact, when I first met you, weren't you dating someone?"

"Not really." Not that she'd ever tried to explain that to him—how she wanted so badly for Sam to think her worthy of his attention that she'd let him believe a casual acquaintance was more. "He was just a friend. I know you had the wrong impression, but I didn't think it would matter." Hadn't believed it would matter, if she told the whole truth. But she so hoped Sam would care.

"Really?" He stopped, holding out his arm.

She took the opportunity to catch her breath. They might not have been going fast by his standards, but for her, the pace was close to a sprint.

"And all this time I could have asked you out, and you never told me?"

So much for trying to get her breath. When she could make her jaw close in a normal manner, she stammered, "You wanted to ask me out?"

"The thought crossed my mind." He grinned. "But you got into all the therapy stuff with me—"

"I'm not a therapist."

"No, but you did a lot better job for me than the guy the state appointed."

"I know." And even though her breathing slowed, her heart hadn't. He'd wanted to ask her out when they'd met. What was stopping him now?

She really needed to get home and indulge in a

good, long cry.

"Look, I'm getting really tired. I'm going home, OK?" She swung toward her street, thankful that she had only a few blocks to go before she reached her haven.

"I'll walk you."

"No, that's OK. You were on your way somewhere else. You go take care of business or whatever. I'll see you later." She bent her head and dug into shoving her crutches in front of her as fast as she could manage.

⌒∽⌒

Sam stared after Robin, his heart shattered. What was wrong? What had he done this time? Here he'd been set to finally ask her out, and she'd taken off like he'd shown her candy and asked her to climb into his car.

Like he was the villain.

Probably because he'd been so clueless about Grace. Why couldn't he just keep his mouth shut about those things? Robin probably thought he agreed with Grace, that no guy would want her because she needed crutches and leg braces to get around.

And what was with her calling herself a cripple? So she used those crutches. She didn't need to demean herself like that. He knew for a fact plenty of other people treated her like an imbecile, as though any disability translated into a mental one, but he'd never seen her give in to it.

He watched her until she turned a corner. Then he came to and looked at the tourists around him. Visitors had fallen off somewhat since the kidnappings, and he was glad to see so many people out today enjoying the sunshine and typical offshore southern California weather, even if most of them were not children. He had seen a few. It might be almost the end of October, but he'd seen some kids playing on the beach, dancing in and out of the waves.

His cell chirped and he grabbed it, hoping it was Robin, calling to ask him to come by after all, that she was sorry for having run off on him, that she wanted to make up.

It was his friend from the police department, Bricker.

"Just thought you should know. It's going to be all over pretty soon—another kid and her babysitter's gone missing."

He closed his eyes, his heart crying out to God when he didn't know how to pray. "Who are they?"

"Cynthia Maxwell is the little one. She's two. The babysitter is a college student, home for a few weeks. Her name is..." Sam heard him fumbling with paper. "Kaitlyn George. I've got a picture on my cell. I'll forward it to you after we hang up."

Sam held the phone against his ear and stared at the oblivious tourists. The sun had turned bitter. The wind that played with fallen leaves became a harbinger of fear.

"Are they putting together search parties?"

"Why I'm calling you. Come help us until you have to report for your shift."

"I'm on my way."

❧❦

Becca stared while the little girl cried and cried and didn't stop. Becca tried to pat her head after Mr.

Bird left, but the baby hit her arm and that made Becca want to cry, too. Except crying made Mr. Bird mad, and she never knew when he was going to come back and catch her. She sure didn't like to make him mad.

If this baby kept crying, and he came back…

Becca sat on the edge of the mattress and cooed, just like her mommy did when she was scared. The baby stopped making noise for a minute, even though her face was still wet, and big fat tears still rolled down her red cheeks. After a minute, she crawled over to where Becca sat, and laid down next to her, with her head in Becca's lap.

That wasn't so nice because her bottom smelled bad, but it was a lot better than all the noise she was making before. Becca laid down, too, and put her thumb in her mouth.

For the first time, she didn't scrape at the hole. Maybe this baby was God's way of making her behave.

But when she woke up later, the baby and her fat tears and stinky bottom were gone.

Mr. Bird came back a long time later.

"Where's the baby?" Becca asked. "I bet she got to go home to her mommy." She felt her lower lip push out, and Mr. Bird didn't like her to pout. She covered her face.

He sat next to her and handed her a sandwich. Peanut butter again. Never with jam. She had to hide another pout.

"She was going to help me, just like you, but it didn't work out. She didn't smell very good, anyway."

The trash didn't smell good, either. Maybe Mr. Bird didn't care about trash smell, though.

Becca opened the sandwich, just to check to see if there might be some jam hidden inside. There wasn't.

"She cried a lot, too. You don't like crying."

He gave her the kind of look her kindergarten teacher used whenever she remembered the name of a letter. "That's right. I don't. You're very smart."

That made her feel better. She took a bite of sandwich and, sucking hard so the peanut butter didn't make her mumble her words, said, "When do I get to help you?"

"Not for a while. I'm telling a story. Your part is way at the end."

"What's the story?"

"It's about my little bird. My sweet, baby-blue-eyed bird."

"Tell me."

He frowned and shook his head. "Not right now. I need to work some of it out, still. Maybe later. When it's your turn to help, I'll tell you everything."

She finished her sandwich and went to the bathroom to run water into her hand, to drink. When she came out, Mr. Bird had gone again. She didn't like how he did that, how he left when she wasn't looking.

She lay down, and right away one thumb went into her mouth and the other hand went to the hole.

If God wanted her to be good, He'd send her another baby to take care of. He couldn't expect her to be good all on her own.

5

Bricker stopped next to Sam, his hands on his hips, as Sam surveyed the old warehouse. Bricker had taken to wearing his uniform, weapon included, every time they searched. It gave the two of them added authority, although the armband the volunteers wore, proclaiming them official searchers, was enough for Sam.

"It's crossed off the list," Bricker said.

"I don't know." Sam stared at the row of windows so dirty they appeared gray.

"We did. In fact, two teams went through, remember?"

"Yeah, I do. But I've got a feeling." He didn't explain it.

"So you want to go in again? Fine, you go. I'm not wasting my time." Bricker turned away, skirting the building and kicking aside boxes and debris in the alley that ran between the warehouse and the service area of a hotel.

Sam pried open the crooked door enough to slip inside. The windows allowed very little light, and he thumbed his flashlight on, sweeping the beam across the gritty floor.

Both he and Bricker, as well as the other team, had been thorough in their searches. *God, am I crazy? Am I wasting time?*

The killer had left Lehanie out in the open. He'd

wanted people to find her. He'd wanted to show off his work. So why did Sam have such a strong urge to look again among the hidden, and the trash? *Guide me, Father.*

A rat scuttled from a pile of boxes, and Sam directed the light toward the corner. Something had shifted them. Not the other team. They'd gone through before Sam. But something—something that interested a rat.

A lot of rats. Three more fled before his light. He heard much scurrying, and several boxes fell as he watched.

Oh, dear God, please.

He crept forward, shoving empty cartons out of his way with his foot, making sure nothing he wanted to find could be hiding in them. After all, Cynthia was only two.

The smell hit him with sudden intensity. Not a dead body, but feces. He stared down at the diaper ripped from the back, chewed by rats, and the chubby leg protruding, and jerked out his phone. "Bricker, get in here. I found the baby."

Setting the flashlight on the edge of a box, so the child could see him as well as he could her, he squatted next to her. "Hey, Cynthia."

"Mommy!" she wailed.

"I know. We're gonna take you to your mommy right now."

She held out her arms, and he reached for her. No matter how disgusting her condition, he could not deny her the comfort of loving arms, hands that wouldn't hurt, hands that didn't want to paint her or kill her.

And he could only thank God that he found her

before the rats finished with the diaper.

৵৽

He watched Sam carry the kid out. Fair enough. It'd be a wasted death if they hadn't found her. For half a minute, he wished her back. He could do her hair and eyes just like he'd done Lehanie's and put her in one of the sky blue outfits he loved and set her up with some stuffed mermaids.

But he couldn't have done that yet. It would give too much away. Better to let this one go and find another little girl for later. There were plenty of babies on the island.

And there was always Becca.

He nodded sharply, once, and headed for home. Becca was at home.

He almost forgot the kid had been found, until he heard the celebrating. He ran toward the crowd, whooping and hollering with the rest of them. He felt someone staring at him, but the best way to avoid suspicion, he'd found, was to ignore it.

He clapped Sam on the back, congratulated him, and let everyone there assume he was as surprised as they were.

No problem. There were plenty of other kids wandering around.

৵৽

Clouds dimmed the day but not the players' faces the next Saturday. Robin looked at each team member in turn as they gathered around Coach Danny for the opening prayer. Robin reached out for Kerry's hand on one side, and Sam covered her fingers, clutched on her crutch, on the other. She bent her head, and a sharp, chill breeze tugged at the hair already clasped in a barrette at the back of her head.

Sam's grip tightened and relaxed, and she glanced at him. His lips tipped up at the corners, more reassurance than actual happiness. But then, she could tell he was worried.

Danny's voice rose and even the squirmiest of players stopped talking. "We ask Your will for our teammates today, that they have fun, that they're good sportsmen, that You keep them safe. But Lord, more than this we ask Your blessings for Kaitlyn George and for little Becca. Follow them. Keep them safe. Bring them home today to their families. And as always, we ask that You keep all our children safe. We ask this in Your name, Amen."

Kerry whooped and headed for the dugout.

Sam leaned close to Robin. "Danny should have been a preacher."

"I think he was, once. He's said a few things that make me think he was, anyway. Or studied to be one." Robin tightened her hold on her crutches and started for the outfield.

"He sure knows how to pray."

Robin watched him in between navigating the hummocks of grass and dirt. "You're doing your best."

He frowned. "What's that got to do with how the coach can pray?"

As if she couldn't read his every expression. "Nothing. It's what you're worried about, though, isn't it?"

He didn't answer, just slipped his mitt over his fist and glared at home base.

Robin stopped beside him and snagged her mitt from his back pocket. She'd never caught anything with it, not yet, but it had already molded itself around her hand. "Look, Sam, you're not responsible for the universe. You found that baby. How can you say you haven't done enough? She would have died if you hadn't found her." She made him meet her gaze, glaring her affirmation into his soul until he looked down, and nodded. "You're not the only one God can use, but then, neither is Danny. He's using us all, anyone who lets Him." She shrugged. "Maybe even the people who don't want Him to. He can use anything, can't He?"

A smile twisted up one side of his mouth. "He sure can."

"So now you're taking a break. Did you even sleep last night?"

"Yeah." His shoulders slumped. "I couldn't help it. I sat down to eat a sandwich and woke up with mustard on my face."

"That must have been pleasant."

"But Becca and Kaitlyn are still out there at the mercy of some sicko. Becca's only five."

"I know, Sam. We all know that. And everyone is doing what they can. Those of us who can't search are praying."

"Yeah, we need prayers." He closed his eyes, probably lost in a prayer of his own for a few minutes. Robin let him do that work in silence. He'd feel better for it.

"Batter up!" Coach Danny's voice echoed across the field.

Robin turned to face the game. "If anyone hits a fly, I want to try to catch it, OK?"

"You got it, babe."

Her lips pinched, but she didn't let him catch her expression. Maybe he didn't know how it sounded. Maybe he didn't mean to ram the word so deep in her heart she'd probably never be able to remove it, never be able to forget it. *Babe.* Like she was his, belonged to him, was beloved by him.

I am Your beloved, that should be enough, shouldn't it?
Sometimes it actually was.

❧❦

Several parents took their kids home as soon as the game ended. The pizza parlor wasn't any less noisy, but Sam still felt the yawning void that their absence left. He settled Kerry next to Robin, bent to tuck her crutches under the table where they wouldn't trip anyone up and rose to find Donovan seating himself across from them. Sam clenched his fists.

Robin wasn't interested in Donovan. She'd made that clear.

But Sam couldn't stop disliking the guy. He sure didn't want to explore how deep the dislike ran, find out if it had progressed to hatred. Or why.

Donovan set his camera next to the parmesan. "I got some good pictures out there today."

Sam took a deep breath and ordered himself to at least be polite. "You got all the permission slips signed?"

"All but a couple. I made sure not to get those kids in the shots. Not too hard, really. And both of those have gone home. Parents thought they'd be safer there, I guess."

"Do you blame them?" Sam met the other guy's

gaze, and let the challenge shine clear in his own.

"Oh, not at all. They want to protect their kids. It's just—what harm can a few pictures do? Or a slice of pizza, you know? It's not like anyone can get to a kid here." He shook his head and mumbled something about parents being overprotective. "We're all here. How's he gonna get to the kid?"

"You never know. It could happen in the bathroom, in five minutes. Destroy a kid's life forever." Sam felt glued to the spot, unwilling to leave Robin and Kerry to this guy, even for the short time it would take to fetch their drinks.

"What, kidnapping? They'd have to get them out—"

"I'm talking about molestation. Isn't that why monsters kidnap kids and kill them after?"

Donovan stared at him, his mouth hanging open before shaking his head. "Yeah. I was just talking about kidnapping."

"It's all related." Sam moved so the server could put the hot pan on the trivet in the center of the table.

Danny, maybe sensing his tension, brought over a pitcher of soda and a stack of cups and plastic lids. He leaned close to Sam's shoulder. "Tone it down, boy. I don't want you starting something in front of the team."

"Right." But the word had to fight past his clenched jaw. Sam pointed at the pizza in the middle of the table and motioned to Donovan. "After you."

"Thanks." Donovan slid two pieces onto his paper plate.

Sam gave both Kerry and Robin a slice.

"Mmm, pepp'roni. My favorite." Kerry took a huge bite, gasping as the hot cheese hit his tongue.

Sam held his soda for him before he filled his own plate.

"Not every kidnapper wants to have—" Donovan stopped, his eyes going to Kerry's face. His own reddened. "They're not all pedophiles. And this guy, he's not even after kids, anyway."

"Are you kidding?" Sam gripped the edge of the table. "You can't be serious. He went after two little girls. No one can find Becca. Why else would—"

"Hey, guys, not here, OK?" Robin put her hand on top of Sam's. He turned his palm up and grasped her fingers.

"Sorry. Inappropriate, I know."

"Very. And we've already been over this once." Robin motioned for another slice and Sam served her. "Thanks. Tell me about the pictures you took at today's game, Donovan. What are you going to do with them?"

Sam turned to see what Donovan would answer.

The other man's jaw bunched over clenched teeth and his eyes narrowed. "Look, I hate pedophiles. Jerks that prey on kids for that—they're sick, they deserve to be put to death. I think that should be the law." He wiped his mouth with the back of his hand. "They ought to be obliterated off the face of the earth. Just put all of them into one of those Nazi ovens and—"

"Donovan. Cool it." Coach Danny dropped his hand onto Donovan's shoulder and shot Sam a look. "We understand your passion but this isn't the place to air it."

"Yeah." Donovan closed his eyes and bent his head. "Yeah, you're right. Sorry."

Danny's fingers tightened so Donovan's t-shirt bunched in wrinkles underneath. "Tell me. You helping in the search for that girl? I know Sam's been out with the search every day since Kaitlyn disappeared."

Donovan looked up. "The first day. I was there when Sam pulled the little kid out of that warehouse."

Sam didn't remember him. But then, there'd been hundreds of people the first day.

Danny let his hand fall. "They still need volunteers. People have lives; they need to get back to their jobs. Why don't you go and see what you can do to help?"

"Yeah, that's a good idea." Donovan slugged back the rest of his soda and stumbled to the door.

Danny watched him go, his shoulders twitching. "He's a good guy, but he needs to put a lock on his mouth."

After a short, tense silence, Robin turned to Kerry. "Hey, buddy, here's a couple quarters. Go play some games for me, all right?"

Kerry's eyes never left Robin's face. "You sure it's OK?"

"Yeah, it's OK. We're here. We'll watch out for you."

"K. Good. K." Kerry got up, lurched a few steps away and turned back. "Thanks, Robin."

She grinned. "You're welcome, my friend."

A short while later, Sam's phone went off. He checked the caller ID before he opened it. "Albrecht here."

"It's Bricker. You know that girl with the crutches?"

Sam glanced to where Robin chatted with a mother of one of her teammates. "Are you talking about Robin?"

At the sound of her name, she glanced up at him, eyes guarded.

"Yup. What's her last name? And while we're at it, what color are her eyes? They're blue, right?"

"Why?"

Bricker let the silence stretch out so that Sam itched to touch Robin's arm, to make sure she was still next to him, alive and well. He didn't. Instead, he turned to block more of the restaurant noise and said, "Yes, they're blue. Why?"

"The girl who went missing three days ago? Kaitlyn? We found her." He didn't sound happy about it.

Sam muttered a word he wasn't supposed to let the kids hear. His heart cried, but he kept the sound from his voice.

"And the perp not only dyed her hair black and painted her eyelids; he made her a cute little pair of crutches, just like your friend's. Out of twigs and some twine, stuff like that."

Revulsion roiled in Sam's gut. "Someone's stalking her?" He checked to see if any of the kids, or worse, Robin, had heard. She stared at him.

"Yeah. Looks like someone's got a nasty, unhealthy obsession with her."

"You got that right." Sam gripped the phone so tight his hand trembled.

"Do you know where Robin is right now?"

"We're both here at Octavio's."

"Can you get her over to the station? We'd like to talk to her."

Robin clasped both shaking hands over her mouth. If she didn't, she'd scream. Or throw up. The gray walls and linoleum of the police station seemed to shriek of coldness and despair, and the questions Officer Bricker kept firing at her exacerbated the effect.

She turned to Sam. "This is bizarre. I'm freaking out here. Who'd *do* that?" She rode over his reassurances without hearing one. "If he wants me, he'd better come after *me*, and leave everyone else alone!"

Bricker leaned closer, blocking her view. "Miss Ingram, I realize this is quite a shock, but we're going to need a list of all the people you know, even casually."

She nodded, nodded again, and said, "I'm sorry. What did you say?"

"A list." Sam pulled her closer to his shoulder. Ever since they'd told her, he'd stuck right next to her. That had been all that was keeping her sane. The minute he left, she wasn't sure what would happen.

"A list of people I know?"

"Everyone." Bricker flipped to a new page in his memo book. "And when you think of someone else, you call me and we'll check them out, too."

"You're going to investigate all my friends? Take them in to question them?"

"Question them all, yes. Take them in if we feel we have reason."

She clenched her hands. "It wasn't a friend of mine who did this. I couldn't love someone like that!"

Sam put his arm around her and kept her grounded. "Even people you know from the grocery store. From your physical therapy group. From the team. Church. People who come into the shop.

Anybody, Robin, it could be anybody."

"Then why—"

"Anybody, yes," the officer interrupted. "But most likely someone you know."

Robin swallowed and closed her eyes. "That does not make me feel good."

Bricker didn't answer.

Robin took a deep breath and started to rattle off names. After a minute, she added, "You can get a list of the team members from Danny. He's got it on his computer, and their phone numbers and families."

Bricker nodded.

Sam said, "I'm not sure everyone is on the list. I mean, people show up to watch, but they're not official runners or even family."

Bricker nodded. "Got it. We'll get started as soon as we can."

"Hey." Sam reached for her arm. "What about that guy Grace keeps talking about? The one who likes you?"

Robin frowned. "What about him?"

"He asks questions about you. And Grace says he likes you."

Bricker looked interested.

Her eyes narrowed and she leaned toward Sam, though she didn't lower her voice. "I thought *you* liked me. We're friends, aren't we? Doesn't that mean *you're* a suspect?"

Bricker stood and shut his memo book. "We're looking into everyone, Miss Ingram. Just because we ask questions doesn't mean we're about to haul anyone off to jail. But we want to stop this guy before he kills again. Remember, there's still a little girl missing."

"Becca Harrison." Robin clasped her arms around

her stomach, trying without success to hold in the chills and the horror. "How could I forget?"

❧❧

Becca kneeled on her mattress and sat back on her heels. In front of her she'd piled every book Mr. Bird had—all seven of them. He'd read all of them to her over and over 'til she could repeat all the words that went with each picture, and in the right order, even when she couldn't see the pictures very well.

Unless Mr. Bird was there with his big old flashlight, the room was almost dark. There was a light bulb right up on the ceiling, but every day the light it gave out got yellower and yellower.

She had lots more books at home, and Mommy and Daddy read those to her over and over, too. But she hadn't heard any of those in so long. She'd kind of forgotten them.

Kind of forgotten Mommy and Daddy, too. She squinted her eyes, half to try to see if she could remember what they looked like, half to keep the tears from falling over her cheeks. Mr. Bird didn't like her to cry. And just because she couldn't remember what Mommy and Daddy looked like, didn't mean she didn't miss them, no matter how nice Mr. Bird was. She remembered how they *felt*. That's what mattered.

The door opened and Mr. Bird pushed a boy in. He was crying and wiping his nose on a muddy sleeve, and he wore some kind of uniform. Becca had seen that kind of uniform on boys at school.

"You're going to sleep in here," Mr. Bird said. "Becca sleeps on the mattress where she's sitting. You can have one of the other ones."

The boy tried to yank away, but Mr. Bird held onto him, tight.

"I don't want to sleep here."

"That's too bad. You're going to have to until your parents come to pick you up." He turned, just like always, and shook the handle of the door, to make sure it was locked.

The boy yelled, "They don't even know where I am!"

"Of course they do. I told them."

"You did not. You kidnapped me."

Mr. Bird's hand crossed the boy's face so fast Becca barely saw it. She shrank back against the side of her mattress, her thumb in her mouth. She'd never seen Mr. Bird do anything like that, even when Lehanie talked back and said all kinds of bad things.

But Lehanie had been a grownup.

Maybe if Becca talked bad to him, he'd hit her, too.

Maybe that word that talked about a kid taking a nap was bad; maybe that was why Mr. Bird got so mad. But it scared her.

No. Mr. Bird liked her lots. He said so over and over. He wouldn't hit her.

It was all the boy's fault. He shouldn't be so nasty.

The boy stopped crying and stared at Mr. Bird with mean, angry eyes.

Becca sucked so hard on her thumb that she made sloppy noises, but no one noticed. She tried to stop. She didn't want Mr. Bird to get mad at her, too.

But Mr. Bird turned away and slammed the door behind him. The boy flew after him, pulling on the knob, but the door wouldn't open.

He stopped after a minute, his shoulders bowed. "What's he gonna do with Simon?"

Becca took her thumb out of her mouth. "Who's Simon?" She wiped her fist on her jeans.

"He's the guy I was canoeing with. My scout leader. That pervert nabbed both of us." He shook his head. "He knocked Simon out and grabbed me. And I don't know what he did with Simon. He made me help him put Simon in a wheelbarrow. Like he was dirt or something." The boy scrubbed the back of his hand across his face and looked at her. "I know who you are. You're Becca Harrison."

She nodded, her eyes wide.

"You're on the news all the time. You and Lehanie. Well, her more, since he killed her."

That made Becca drop her thumb out of her mouth. Mr. Bird said she went home. "Who killed her?"

"That pervert." The boy jerked his thumb toward the door.

Becca shook her head hard. "Uh-uh. She went home. Mr. Bird told me she did a job for him, and she went home. I'm supposed to do one for him, but later. Anyway, Mr. Bird wouldn't hurt anybody." Remembering how Mr. Bird had just slapped the boy, she said, "Not that kind of hurt. Just don't say that bad word anymore. Mr. Bird doesn't like bad words."

"Boy, are you dumb."

"No, I'm not!" Why did Mr. Bird have to put this boy in her room, anyway? She really didn't like him. She hoped Mr. Bird would take him away really fast, like he did with the baby. Or let her do her job so she could go home. She wanted her mom and dad so bad. She couldn't help it, now she started to cry again, and she couldn't stop.

The boy pinched his lips together and didn't say

anything.

Becca rolled onto her stomach and within seconds her fingers were in the hole. She'd have to do it real quiet now, with this kid here. He was so mean, he'd probably tell Mr. Bird and get her in trouble.

Nothing made her feel better, except digging that hole. Digging out little bits of white and more of the paint, and each time she scraped some stuff out of her fingernails and stuck her fingers back in the hole, she felt better.

She used to sing really soft to herself. She wouldn't do that with this mean boy listening. Besides, singing "Jesus Loves Me" never made her feel so good. It made her remember church, and Mommy and Daddy, and made her want to cry, but it didn't make her feel better.

Jesus was supposed to love her. That's what that song was all about. So if He did, why did He take her away from her mommy and daddy?

❧⸎

He stood outside the room, leaning his head against the door. Things were getting too complicated. Sometimes he forgot what the plan was.

He shook his head. Forgetting the plan would be the worst thing.

He wasn't so sure about this kid. Becca was fine; she was a sweetheart. So far, she was the only other person on earth who believed in his vision. But this new kid might be a mistake. Cocky wasn't the word for him. He needed to learn a lesson.

And there he went again, forgetting the plan. Forgetting the perfect vision. He had to concentrate.

He walked away from the door, out of the house,

down the road to the harbor. The water would clear his thinking. It always did. And if he saw *her*, all the better.

Seeing her always helped. It pulled him back to his vision, helped him to see how necessary it was to get the job done.

It wouldn't be long until he made *her* a part of the plan. Now they'd told her about the vision, about the hair and the eyes and the crutches—which she shouldn't have to use—she'd finally understand.

She had to.

6

"Boy scouts?" Sam leaned on the counter and stared at the picture of two boys, arms around each other, grinning at the camera. Both had the required two-fingered rabbit ears behind their heads. Behind them stood a young man proudly wearing scout leader emblems. He'd probably gone straight from his Eagle Scout badge to being an assistant cub master.

"One scout, one scout leader. Simon Carson. His sisters go to the same school my kids do. And now their big brother is missing." His finger smudged across one of the boys. "This is Jake West. He's ten, almost eleven. Fifth grade, a good kid. Dad left a few years ago so he spends a lot of time with the scout leaders. They mentor him."

Sam turned away. "What is wrong with this guy? Now he's after boys? Males? What's he going to do to *them*?" Sam took a breath to choke some of the fury from his voice. None of this was Bricker's fault. But everyone was on edge, everyone spouting off about this pervert. Even Donovan had done his share.

Almost made him like the guy.

Well, maybe not that close to almost.

"Who knows?" Bricker slugged back half a cup of coffee and wiped his face with his hand. "The thing is, he didn't do anything with the girls."

"What are you talking about? He *killed* them, Bricker, two of them, anyway. He played dolls with

Lehanie and—"

"Yeah. All that. But he didn't touch them. No sign of rape."

Sam stared at his friend, finally remembered his mouth hung open. "Why don't people know? Everyone assumes that's why both those girls were—"

Bricker shrugged. "It's one of the things they aren't letting out. But it helps to know."

After a moment, Sam opened his eyes. "Yeah, it does help. But the guy is still a pervert, and we still have to find him." And if Sam were in on the find, he sure hoped God would forgive him for forgetting he was a Christian, just for a minute. That was all he needed. One minute, and the pervert at his mercy.

He shook his head. No matter what, he wouldn't forget. And he had to pray for the resolve to keep himself in check. Or pray that he was far away when they caught him. Pray that if he ever got the chance, he *would* show mercy. Could show it.

He didn't want that, either, not when the guy seemed to be after Robin. Another bit of privileged information, but not something he wanted to dwell on.

"You ready to go back out?"

Sam pushed his cup away and stood. "Yeah. Though I wonder if we'll find these two any faster than we found the other victims." Somehow, it felt safer to refer to Lehanie and Kaitlyn as victims. It made them one word removed from human, and he could breathe.

"Don't be so positive." Bricker led the way outside to where he'd parked his patrol car. Usually the officers weren't allowed to drive them off duty, but that rule had been waived for the searches.

Sam got in the passenger seat, buckled himself, and held onto the window frame as Bricker peeled out of the station lot.

Two days past the time change, it was already dark by five in the afternoon. They passed an empty park, the swings hanging forlorn, and Bricker pulled to the curb.

"Saw something," he yelled as he bolted from the car.

Sam followed. A male figure darted across the open grass. Sam veered away from Bricker, heading at an angle to cut off the now-running man. The guy vaulted over a low concrete wall, and Sam did the same.

His feet slid in a scuff of weeds and gravel. He fell back, skidding on his heels and one protesting hand, down to a ditch that ran between backyards. After pushing himself to his feet, he ran again. The guy was halfway over a wall when Sam caught up to him. He grabbed a jean-clad leg. The booted foot slammed into Sam's jaw, and he stumbled back. He jumped again, caught the boot and tugged. Another kick to his face brought pain. Within seconds warmth flooded over his mouth and onto his shirt. The boot slid from his fingers and the leg disappeared.

"Bricker!" The name came out strangled. He tried again.

In a few seconds, Bricker hopped over the wall behind him.

Sam pointed. "That way." He held one hand to his nose, still pouring blood.

Bricker lumbered over the wall, and Sam sagged against it. He'd lost the guy to a stupid broken nose. If he hadn't been so sure his bloody hands would slip on the chain link he'd have gone after him. He should have anyway. He shouldn't let something like this stop him.

Again.

"Lost him." Panting, Bricker dropped next to him and grabbed Sam's elbow. "Let's get you to the emergency room."

"I let him go."

"What? Can't understand you."

This time Sam enunciated each word. "I let him go."

"Yeah, he broke your nose. I'd have had to do the same thing." Bricker studied him as they trudged across the park. "It wasn't a choice, Sam. He got away. It happens. Even to cops."

But Sam imagined the look in Robin's eyes when he confessed.

∂∼∽

He walked the street without really seeing it, his mind on his last set of pictures. The residential part of town was all cramped together houses, anyway, a few gardens squeezed in, with cheesy nautical ornaments. No true beauty. No wonder they didn't understand his vision. What would it take to make them see?

Someone shouted, "Hi."

He looked up.

That kid Robin liked so much stumbled toward him, waving his only usable arm and shouting something that might have been his name. He glanced around. How easy would it be to lure the kid away, up his secret path? There was no one on the street. No one to point and claim it was him; he's the one.

He hurried up to the kid, making his smile as big and natural as he could get it. A wasted effort, really.

The kid wasn't smart enough to figure things out.

"Hey, Kerry."

"Hi. Hi. Are you going for a walk, too? My mom said I could get licorice." He held up a dollar crumpled in his fist.

A man came around the corner.

No chance now, but it didn't matter. He had his eye on Kerry, now. He remembered how much Robin liked him. He'd make plans.

And he could get to Kerry at any time.

෧ஓ

The next Wednesday, Robin and Sam met again for lunch.

Robin took the cold bottle of Italian cherry soda Sam handed her and watched him slump on the bench next to her.

Putting the mouth of his bottle to his lips, he took a long pull. He still wore the bits of bandage over his nose, and drinking looked painful.

But he wouldn't talk about the incident, only looked murderous when she brought it up. So she didn't. He'd talk about it when he was ready, and if he never was, well, time would heal some of the pain.

When he put down the bottle, he stared away from her, and Robin followed his gaze across the bay.

Wind whipped white froth off the tips of the waves, so it looked like snow topping glassy turquoise and greens, and wafted seagulls into a gentle dance under a few clouds.

"Looks like paradise, doesn't it?"

"Always. I love this island."

She unwrapped the packet of sandwiches, handed

one over, and pulled a bag of oatmeal and raisin cookies from her backpack. Now to make another judgment call—ask or keep silent. But silence wasn't her game, and it never helped anyone as far as she knew. She took a deep breath. "What's wrong, Sam?"

He stiffened and shrugged. "Nothing, really. I just got done talking to Kerry's mother."

"Why? What happened?" The muscles in her back tensed and her shoulders snapped into a straight line. She could take on whatever bad news Sam had for her. She had to, even when it came to Kerry.

"Hey, it all turned out all right." Sam put his hand on her knee. Something that felt like warm honey trickled through her veins. "Kerry's fine. But you know how trusting he can be." Sam glanced up, the pain in his eyes almost flattening her.

"Oh, no." Her whisper barely made it to her own ears. She doubted Sam could have heard her, but he must have read her expression.

"He's OK, Robin. Yeah, he nearly got snagged by the creep, but someone saw." Sam bent his head. "If I'd caught that guy the other night, this probably wouldn't have happened, but God covered for me."

"You don't know it was the same guy, Sam. The guy who got away might have just lifted some tourist's wallet. You don't *know*."

Head shaking, Sam re-wrapped his sandwich. He hadn't even taken a bite.

"Who helped him? Whoever it is deserves a reward."

Sam sighed. "Oh yeah. Believe it or not, Donovan's the one who rescued him. The creep got away, but both Kerry and Donovan got a look at him so the police put together a sketch, and they're going to publish it tonight. Well, I gather Kerry was pretty confused, but Donovan was really specific. So now we have an idea of who we're looking for." He stared at her.

Robin wanted to point out that if Donovan had rescued Kerry, he couldn't be all bad. But she let it go. Sam had to realize that Donovan had some good qualities now, but she wouldn't make him admit it out loud. She'd give him that much pride.

"I'm going to go talk to his mom. Kerry shouldn't be out alone for a while." She rewrapped her own sandwich and put it, along with Sam's, back into her pack. "Come with me? We can offer to sort of—not babysit. He's too old for that, but we've got to do something."

"I agree." Sam stood and helped her pull her backpack over her shoulders. "Be his back for as long as he needs us."

She fitted her crutches to her arms and gripped them hard. The walk to the Wright's house was farther than she'd planned to go, and she always had to portion out her energy to last the day. But Kerry meant more to her than a bad afternoon.

"Why don't we go get your cart?" Sam asked.

"It's not charged." She made a face. "I forgot to plug it in last night."

He didn't move for a minute before he pulled out his cell phone. After a short conversation, he smiled. "Kerry's mom will bring him down here. Really. Anyway, Kerry always likes to take a walk, and that'll give his mom something to do with him."

"What? Kerry can walk that far, but I can't?"

His mouth went tight and straight and his eyes narrowed. "Will you stop being so doggone proud?

There's some things you can't do. So what? Get over it." He flipped his phone open and jabbed at the keypad.

Robin sat down, her cheeks burning. That told her what he thought of her. If it weren't for Kerry, she'd go home. If it weren't for her crutches, she'd run away.

Ten minutes later, during which neither of them ate any of the lunch Robin had provided, and neither of them spoke, Mrs. Wright trudged down the hill with Kerry next to her. Usually he was either a few feet behind or a few feet in front. Today, it looked like she'd threatened him to keep him as close as possible. He didn't even smile when Sam said hi.

As soon as his mother let go of his hand, he lumbered to the bench where Robin sat and plopped next to her. "I can't go anywhere. I can't go to the park 'cept on team day, and I can't go for a walk or nothing. I can't go to Ray's house. I can't do *anything* by myself." His eyes and tone told the whole saga of injustice.

"We're going to help with that." Robin put her arm around his stiff shoulders. "Sam and I are going to hang out with you whenever we can."

Kerry looked from Sam's face to Robin's, still frowning. "Can we go places?"

"Sure." Not that Avalon offered an array of entertainment, other than for the tourists, but Kerry wouldn't know that. He'd grown up on the island, just like Robin had, and as far as she knew, he'd seldom been off.

"Will you take me for rides in your golf cart?"

Robin laughed. "Sure." At least one person in the world saw her as something more than a cripple. She glowered at Sam for half a second and decided to let the anger go. He probably hadn't meant to hurt her. He thought he was being realistic.

Mrs. Wright wriggled Kerry's hand. "Did you hear that, Kerry? Now you can have a little more freedom with either Robin or Sam."

He twisted to face his mother. "And Donovan."

"Oh, sure. You can go places with Donovan. That's fine. But he hasn't offered to take you anywhere."

"But he saved me." Kerry's limbs tightened with his excitement. "Did you hear 'bout that? Donovan saved me. An old creep was trying to make me go with him, but Donovan wouldn't let him."

"His new hero." Mrs. Wright chuckled. "Really, I feel a lot better knowing you two are willing to take on Kerry."

Sam opened his mouth, but Robin interrupted. "We're not taking him on." Not as if he were a burden, anyway. "We're doing a favor. And we like hanging out with Kerry."

"'Cuz we're friends, remember, Robin? You always said we're friends. No matter what."

"That's right." She gave him a one-armed hug.

❧❧

The next day, as Robin entered the co-op, Grace leaned on the counter and watched Robin drag herself onto the stool behind the counter. "You looked wiped out. What's up?"

Robin ran a hand through her hair, gathered it, and wrapped a band around it. "Sam and I talked to Kerry's mom and set up a schedule so he doesn't have to go places alone for a while."

"Kerry's a grown man."

"Yeah, well, some creep tried to grab him. We're not taking any chances. Even Kerry sees the sense in that. He knows he needs to be protected."

Grace shrugged and pulled a box of merchandise from under the counter. "So how'd he get away from the predator?"

"Remember Donovan? The photographer?"

Grace stared at Robin, her mouth open in exaggerated shock, a handful of ceramic dolphins dangling from her fingers. "Do I? Honey, the woman who could forget him is dead."

Robin grimaced. "Well, he saw what happened and ran after the guy. Chased him off. It would have been better if he'd stopped him, got the police or something. But at least Kerry is OK."

"So on top of being beautiful, this guy is a knight in shining armor, and you're still not interested?"

"Looks aren't everything."

Grace grinned. "No. Which is why I mentioned the knight part."

"He's a nice guy. There just isn't anything there."

"Because of Sam."

"Because I'm not interested!"

"He is." Grace peered at Robin from under her bangs. "Remember all the toys he bought? All *your* toys? The ones he mailed to Michigan, for his nieces."

Robin stared at her friend, trying to keep her voice as level as her gaze. "Sure, I remember. And I told you that was nice of him."

Grace planted her hands on her hips. "Is that all you can say?"

"I'm not interested. He's nice, he's good looking, and he does nothing for me." She settled onto the rolling stool and edged toward the counter.

"But maybe you should—"

"What?" Robin spun, leaning forward, her hands clenched. "Settle for him because he's the only guy interested in me?"

Tsking, Grace said, "It's not settling when a guy looks like that."

Robin shook her head. "I can't convince you, can I?"

"I just think you're missing out on something really good."

Robin closed her eyes to keep the tears from showing. "I know. I am. But it's not Donovan I'm missing."

7

The pizza parlor was as noisy as ever, more because of the video games begging for players than the number of patrons. Sam looked around the restaurant. "You'd think more parents would be bringing their kids to places like these."

"Are you kidding?" Robin edged around the end of a bench.

Sam knew better than to offer help. The last time he'd suggested getting a special chair for her, so she wouldn't have to maneuver the benches, she hadn't talked to him for a week. Add her reaction when he'd insisted Kerry do the walking instead of Robin, and he might end up without a best friend. Better to let her play Miss Independent and stick around to pick up the pieces if he ever needed to. So far, he hadn't. She seemed to know her own limits better than he did.

In fact, he was the one who tended to end up in pieces, each time he offended her pride.

Sam shook his head. Worrying about Robin in front of her would not help his case, so instead, he concentrated on the subject. "What's wrong with bringing kids here? It's safe. There's only one exit."

Donovan bumped past Sam and slid next to Robin, leaving Sam no place but across the table from her. "There's the bathroom." He glowered at Sam. "You're the one who pointed out what a guy could do to a kid in a bathroom, and how quick it can happen. And you're right." He shook his head. "I used to think people were being paranoid, you know? Until I saw that guy go after Kerry. If I were a parent, I'd make my kid wear diapers until he graduated high school."

Robin's face showed her revulsion, but Donovan didn't see it. Sam did, though, and his spirits rose. He tried not to smirk. "I'd be more careful. Stand outside the door, check the place out first. But kids have to have some fun sometime."

"Sure they do. But not when there's some monster out there just waiting to molest them." His face contorted. "They oughta just castrate those guys the minute they see they've got any sort of inclination to that."

Robin smacked her forehead. "Donovan, please, not again. There are children here."

Sam, studying Robin's face, thought, *and young women with tender hearts*. He reached across the table and covered her hand with his.

Donovan glared at her. "What do you want to do, Robin, throw our kids in his way without telling them what could happen to them?"

"I don't think they need details."

Sam gripped her hand as she jerked.

Donovan stood, his jaw trembling. "I'm only thinking about the kids. No one wants to see molesters killed better than me. No one." He jerked out his wallet, threw a twenty on the table and strode out.

Robin bent and covered her face with her hands. "I'm sorry. I just don't think the kids need graphic details. Not of what could happen, and not of what he'd do to the criminals who'd do it."

Sam squeezed her hand before he let go and reached for the food in front of him. "But they need to know what to avoid."

I'm not arguing that." She rubbed her face and finally dropped her hands to her lap. "I just don't agree with his methods."

"You have to admit, he's passionate about it."

"Right." She didn't seem impressed.

Should he point out how completely they'd each taken the other's position, him defending Donovan, her lambasting him? But no. He'd just enjoy it while it lasted. He went around the table and hugged her gently. "You can't fault him for that."

"I guess. But most people get pretty upset about pedophiles." She pushed a stray lock of black hair behind her ear and shrugged out of his embrace.

Sam grinned, but only as he went back to his place across the table from her. No sense giving her a reason to stop talking to him again. "That, too. I mean, I feel the same way."

"Can we talk about something else?"

"Anything you want, Robin. Anything you want."

❧❦

Robin watched Sam over the rim of her soda cup. He was a lot nicer when Donovan wasn't around. He might not love Robin, not in the way that meant the most to her, but he sure didn't want Donovan playing up to her either. Not that Donovan had tried much today. He'd taken a few team pictures, wandered around the edge of the field and watched, mostly. Donovan was a nice enough guy, but he made her nervous. And that was probably Grace's fault, with her constant pushing to get Robin to go out with him, when he hadn't even asked.

Outside the parlor, after lunch, Robin hitched her crutches under her arms and edged onto the bus lift. Sam leaned through the door, getting the driver's attention. "Can I get a ride today? There aren't that many kids, and I'm getting off the same place as Robin."

"Against policy." The driver reached for the controls.

Before he could shut the door in Sam's face, Robin said, "Fine, I'll walk."

The driver glared at her and threw Sam a dirty look. "All right, already. Just don't think I'm going to make a habit of this."

"Thanks." Sam bounded onto the bus, waited for Robin to take her seat, and sat across the aisle from her. He leaned toward her, one elbow on his knee, a slight grin on his face. Go figure. He always got what he wanted.

"You're such a player," she told him.

"What?" He straightened, outrage widening his eyes.

"You play people. Maybe I should have said manipulator, but it's not as pithy."

He laughed. "Hey, whatever it takes." Still chuckling, he relaxed against the seat and stretched his arm along it, reaching toward her. "Don't tell me you'd rather have walked. Anyway, you were the one who persuaded him."

"Only because you wanted me to."

"I never said that."

"Not in words."

For a long moment he studied her face. His gaze felt like a warm glow washing over her, just like his touch. Exotic, enticing, and a little uncomfortable.

She'd never get herself free from him, and he'd never much want her either. And someday, maybe when she hit eighty or so, it would stop hurting.

After several more minutes, he sighed. "You know me too well."

"You say that like it's a bad thing."

He chuckled again, completely without humor and without looking at her. "Depends. This time, maybe. I don't know." He jumped up. "Here's our stop."

She struggled to her feet and clomped down the aisle after him. The driver waited for Sam to land on the street before he engaged the lift. She stepped on it, staggered and wavered for half a second before she pitched off.

Sam caught her, not quite before she hit the ground, but before she'd sustained too much damage. Still, she glared at her right knee, now covered in shredded uniform, grit and flecks of blood, and stinging like crazy.

"Ah, babe." Sam bent to check out her leg and that gave her time to control her reaction to his nickname. Really, he had to stop calling her that. It was killing her. "Think you can make it inside?"

"Yeah, sure." She shifted her crutches and tried not to put as much weight on that leg. She walked funny enough without the extra pain, and hot shame dogged her as closely as Sam, with his outstretched arms and wrinkled brow. He was sweet to be so concerned, but, oh, did he have to see how badly the lower half of her body flopped around, out of her control?

"Do you want to sit down while I wash it off?"

"I think I need to lie down." So much for acting

the stoic. She jabbed her crutch toward her bedroom just off the living room.

Sam was helping her lift herself onto her bed when her grandmother came in. She stood at the door to Robin's room, hands on her hips, and watched. "What happened, kiddo?"

"I fell getting off the bus."

Gram tsked her tongue but came forward to stroke Robin's hair. "I'm really glad I don't have to worry about you having a man in your room."

"I'm not." Oh, but that was the pain talking, pain from the sting of humiliation rather than the scraped knee. She looked at Sam, ignoring her grandmother's hoots of laughter.

His lips twitched.

She'd kill him as soon as she could move.

Gram disappeared and came back a moment later with the first aid kit and a dripping cloth, which she handed to Sam. He wiped at her knee, pausing when she gasped but going on with it.

As soon as her grandmother left them again, Robin said, "I didn't mean—"

"I know what you meant." Sam bent as though he had to see a particularly difficult bit of grit in her wound. "Looks like you're ready for the bandaging." He took care of that and carried the box to her dresser.

Robin lay on her bed, still burning. She wanted him to leave. She wanted the chance to curl on her side and cry. She wanted to replay the conversation until she could convince herself she hadn't said those awful words, but that couldn't happen.

"Pretty curtains." Sam pointed to the waterfall of beads covering her window, which faced the street.

Great. Such an obvious ruse to change the subject.

She bit anyway. "My dad helped me make them."

"Your dad?" His eyebrows headed for his hairline.

"Yeah. The only time I ever saw him. I mean, I probably did when I was tiny, but I don't remember. When I was about three, he had an accident, and he stopped talking. Lots of brain damage. He's been in this home on the mainland since then." It was an old story to Robin, one that hurt and reassured her at the same time.

"But he made curtains for you?"

She nodded and sat up. The pain had eased when he finished bandaging it, and now, the heat that had flooded her chest had cooled. "He got to come here for a month one summer. He brought all these beads with him, all colors of blue and green, colors of the sea. And we spent hours every day stringing beads. Gram said it was his therapy, but for me—"

"It was a connection."

"Yes." She looked up at Sam, at his kind, sweet face, and for half a minute was almost glad she'd let him know how she felt about him. Because love unexpressed was such a waste. "It was our thing. He did it because he loved me, even if he couldn't say the words."

Sam smiled and let the strands trickle through his curled hand. "What a beautiful legacy." When the last string clattered against the baseboard, he turned. "I promised Bricker I'd go with him on another search. We're looking around the foothills. They've covered the whole area between Avalon and Wrigley, but there's acres and acres we haven't touched. Miles." He bent his head. "The two scouts could be anywhere."

"And Becca."

"Right. I hope—"

"You hope she's still alive."

"You got it, yeah. All of them."

"I'll be praying."

"Thanks." He headed for the door, turned back, and dropped a kiss on her cheek.

Only after the front door closed behind him did Robin realize she still had her hand cradled against her face.

❧✦

Sam went with Kerry to meet Robin at the park. He'd left her on a bench and hiked up to Kerry's house to save her the walk. It probably would have been better to take her golf cart. Next time he'd suggest it, no matter what kind of a glare she gave him. Fully able locals used the carts to get around. Why couldn't she?

And it would be better for Kerry, too. He didn't need to wear himself out walking so far.

As the two men got closer, Sam saw what Robin was doing. Three baseballs were lined up on a flat stretch of grass, and she smacked each one with her crutch, as though it were a golf club. She wasn't bad, either.

"Hey, Robin. You should play golf," Kerry yelled. He stumbled forward, and Sam moved close behind him, a hand out in case Kerry lost his balance.

Robin looked up, grinning. "I can drive a mean golf cart, too."

Sam laughed. "You should drive it more often."

She shrugged and handed Kerry one of the balls. "Did you bring your mitt?"

"Sam has it."

Sam produced it from his back pocket, pulled his

own out of the other, and grabbed the aluminum bat from the bench where he'd piled everything. "Are we all ready?"

"Sure. You want to go first, Kerry?"

Kerry grabbed the bat and hunkered over the patch of spiky grass that Robin explained was their make-believe home base. "I'm gonna hit it outta the park!"

"You bet." Sam retrieved all three of the baseballs and waited for Robin to move out of swing distance before he pitched a gentle ball toward Kerry. After a string of hits and even more misses, he took the bat and told Kerry to sit down and drink some water. "You get worn out and your mom won't let you come back." That was enough to make Kerry cooperate, if he had a mind not to.

"Where's the picture guy?" Kerry wiped his drippy mouth on the inside of his shirt. "Why isn't he taking pictures?"

"I think he only comes to the official games." Sam watched Robin as he said it. After her comment to her grandmother a few days before, Sam had gone back and forth about telling the older woman about Donovan. Warning her that the other man wasn't the type she could allow into Robin's room unattended. Not that Robin would forgive him for saying anything like that, but sometimes his need to protect her overrode his need to give her dignity. So far, he hadn't said anything. Let Donovan make one comment, let Robin let on she had changed her mind back to liking the guy, or believing he needed defending, and he would.

Not that he felt completely safe in her room himself. But he didn't want to think about that, not with Robin watching his face, not with Kerry to attend to.

"He takes pictures all the time. He took mine."

"At the game, right?"

"No. After." Kerry wriggled on the bench. "Can I bat again?"

"In a minute. You need to rest some more." Robin patted his shoulder.

And Sam needed to ask more questions. "When did he take your picture? Was your mom there?"

"Nope. I was walking."

"Was that when the creep tried to take you away?"

"No. That was later. He took pictures when Mama let me walk to the store. On Monday. I got licorice."

"OK." So Donovan was going around taking pictures of vulnerable people and that meant—what? Kerry was an adult, legally. "So, does he touch you?"

Robin gaped at him, but Sam ignored her.

"You mean bad touching, right? Nope. Donovan's a good guy, Sam. He's like you. He wouldn't hurt me. He rescued me, remember?"

"Right. I remember."

"When he took me home, he told me all about people who try to hurt other people. Bad people. He said I had to be real careful. He told Mama to watch out for me, and that's why I can't go for walks on my own anymore." He frowned. "Now I can't get licorice."

"OK, OK, I get it. Are you ready to practice some more?"

"Yeah, I'm ready!" Kerry jumped up and grabbed the bat before he went back to the patch of grass Robin had pointed out. "Is this the right place, Robin?"

She glanced over. "It sure is, Kerry. Good eye." She held out her crutch to stop Sam from heading toward Kerry. "You're a jerk."

"What? I just wanted to make sure."

"No, you wanted Kerry to say something so you could blame Donovan for everything."

She held out her hand for the ball and Sam handed it over. And she spent the next ten minutes pitching it at Kerry's bat. If Sam had gotten in the way, he was pretty sure she wouldn't have minded.

8

Every day, Becca would sit on her mattress and watch Jake tap around the floor and pound on the walls, trying to find a way out of Mr. Bird's special room. Jake yelled a lot, too, when he thought Mr. Bird was gone.

Once Mr. Bird heard him, though, and grabbed his ear and dragged him out the door.

Jake didn't yell for a long time after Mr. Bird brought him back.

But Becca had seen the bruises on his face and arms. That scared her so bad. She didn't want to ask if Mr. Bird hit Jake. If he told her yes, that meant she couldn't like Mr. Bird anymore, and if Becca couldn't like him, that meant she didn't have anybody to like.

"You aren't gonna find anything," Becca told him after Jake finished trying to rattle the door open.

"What, you'd rather die?" Jake tried to twist the tops of the door hinges with his fingers. "I want to make him sorry he ever nabbed me and Simon."

"He took your tools." Becca rubbed her eyes, remembering how Jake had howled about losing the things she thought were just Boy Scout toys. "There's nothing you can do."

"That's not true!" Jake looked like a mean dog with his lips pulled up and his teeth showing. "We're gonna get out of here!"

Becca shoved her thumb in her mouth and

slurped. Ever since this boy came, everything had been scary. He made Mr. Bird so mad, and that meant Mr. Bird wasn't nice to Becca anymore. He wouldn't read to her, or hold her. He wouldn't tell her about his robin, his own little bird he loved so much that he would do anything for her. He wouldn't listen when she asked him to tell her the robin story, the one she got to help with later. He brought food, same as always, but he didn't tell stories while she ate. He never answered her when she asked about her mommy and daddy. He didn't care when she cried, not even enough to get mad at her.

She cried a lot now.

It didn't help.

Jake walked around the room, his arms crossed like he wanted to hug himself. Every so often, he'd stop and look up at the ceiling, or at the concrete floor, or the walls that had no windows, or the light way above their heads, that never went out. And he'd shake his head.

Becca laid down on the bed and put her thumb back in her mouth. Her other hand went down between the mattress and the wall. The hole was bigger now, bigger than her whole hand even when she spread her fingers out. If Jake found it, he'd tell Mr. Bird. Or maybe not. But if it got too big, Mr. Bird would find out anyway.

She didn't want Mr. Bird to drag her out by her ear and do things to her. Spank her maybe.

And she still couldn't help digging into the crumbly white stuff. The feel of it under her nails, and the feel of her thumb in her mouth, made everything better, safe, and she dug until she fell asleep.

❦❧

"I feel guilty coming out here to have fun when those kids are still missing." Robin adjusted her grip on her crutches. For their foray across the sand, she'd slipped x-cut tennis balls over the tips. Though they kept the crutches from sinking too far into the sand, they did nothing to protect her braces. Those, she knew, would fill with irritating particles and chafe her shins long before she got to where she could take them off. Still, time on the beach was more than worth the irritation.

Sam reached for her elbow but moved back. "Not having fun won't help them."

"But we could be doing something."

"We have been." This time Sam grabbed her as she teetered but let go once she'd regained her balance. "I've been out with Bricker almost every day. You're praying. You're collecting funds at the co-op. You're cooperating with the police. You're doing everything you can. And we both deserve a break." His gaze cut to her. "Robin, we've been over this. You're not doing anything wrong."

She nodded, concentrating on dragging each foot after the other. The resistance as the sand piled up made her slower than ever. She glanced up at Sam.

He looked across the water. His eyes squinted against the never-ending wind, but she didn't get the impression of impatience from his posture. Instead, he had shoved his hands in his pockets and seemed content to take one long, leisurely step to every three of her shuffles.

She stopped to catch her breath, and he nodded toward the beach. "You can see the mainland today."

She peered toward the horizon where a long, low smear of shadow bisected the sea and sky. "Pretty cool to see something that's twenty-six miles away."

"And they can see us."

"You suppose anyone's looking? Even here, there aren't too many people on the beach."

His gaze made a lazy arc before it stopped on her. "It's the end of October. Probably as cold there as it is here. But I'll bet there's someone out there as excited with the clear sky as we are."

Robin nodded and took another few shuffles. At this rate, she'd never reach the water. And when she did, she'd collapse from exhaustion.

Again, Sam scanned the beachfront and turned to her, grinning. "Want a piggyback ride?"

She pulled up short, wobbling until she plunked a ball-covered crutch tip deep into a sand valley. "What?"

"You'll get there faster."

"You want to rush down to the water, feel free." She bent her head to hide her eyes, but the wind whipped her hair away and exposed her anger.

"That's not my point. You're already breathing hard. Look, it doesn't have to mean anything, Robin. It'll be like I'm your runner. Just helping out where you need it."

That was it? He just wanted to help, and she could accept it on the baseball field but not here? Robin bit her lip and stared at her crutches. She could remember back to when she didn't have them, when people, usually her grandmother, carried her everywhere she needed to go. She hadn't started taking steps until she was almost five, after her fourth or fifth surgery.

She could even remember back to when her

mother carried her—here, to this island, to leave her once and for all, complaining about Robin's weight and saying that she wasn't even trying.

Robin had been trying ever since, but now, maybe that meant trying Sam's patience. He only wanted to help, and he never—almost never—invaded her space or forced his help on her. He asked, and he respected her decisions.

Refusing just made it harder on both of them.

"All right."

A wider grin transformed his face. Before, it had been pleading. Now, he was just happy. And rather than haul her to his back, he scooped her up, crutches and braces and all, and strode to the water's edge. He let her down, bent, and untied one of her shoes. "Step up." He didn't look at her but remained in a squat, waiting.

She lifted her foot high enough that he was able to slip the shoe off. He unlocked the brace, loosened all the straps, and let it fall.

When she let her bare foot touch the sand she remembered the feel of it—gritty and warm from the hidden sun, almost silky and yet full of sensuous texture.

He started to work on her other foot before she realized it, and within seconds that shoe and brace were off as well. Sam stood. "Leave your crutches, too. Don't worry. I won't let you fall." He gathered her in his arms, with the same clinical detachment he used as her runner, and carried her to the water.

Oh, it was cold, freezing, delicious and foamy and full of the scent of fish and salt.

She closed her eyes against the wind and immediately felt as though she were moving. The breeze rushed her body as did the waves. When the water changed direction, she had to open her eyes so as not to get dizzy.

Sam let go of her legs, and she set her feet on the sand, let the waves pull at them, pull them out from under her. He had such a tight grip on her that she knew she wouldn't collapse, would never float away from him.

They played in the waves for half an hour before Sam turned her to look into her eyes. "You're worn out. Let's go back."

She nodded and let him carry her up through the encroaching tide and across the expanse of sand.

He set her on a concrete wall and went back for her things. Before he slid the braces back on her legs, he dried her skin with the edge of his t-shirt and brushed away every speck of sand, both from her legs and the braces. Each time his fingers touched her, she shivered.

"Won't be too long," he said. "Pretty soon we'll get you home where it's warm."

It was while he was putting her shoes back on, and tying the laces, that someone stopped next to them.

Robin looked up.

Donovan stood with his camera around his neck. He hadn't seemed to notice Robin yet, but his expression as he looked down at Sam puzzled her.

"Donovan," she said.

Sam straightened, though still on his knees in front of her, and looked at the other man.

Donovan gave Robin only half a glance before he focused again on Sam. "Been playing?"

"Yup. Isn't that what the beach is for?"

Donovan's lips pinched, but he didn't answer. "I

was getting some shots of the mainland from up there"—he pointed toward the top of the cliffs—"when I saw you down here. I wasn't quite sure who you were, Sam. I thought maybe Robin was in trouble, so I wanted to make sure she was all right."

"I'm fine. I'm with Sam. Why wouldn't I be all right?" But Robin heard the crack in her voice, and the two men must have heard it as well.

Donovan finally looked at her. "It just seemed like an odd thing for you to do—go in the water when it's so cold, and rough." When she frowned, he went on, "I was worried. That's all."

"Donovan—"

Sam stood, though one hand still reached to Robin's knee. "I can take care of her, you know. I wouldn't let anyone hurt her."

"I'm right here, you know."

"Of course you are." Sam smiled, his glinting gaze warming as he looked at her. "And I promised to get you home soon, so that's where we're going." He handed her the crutches and nodded to Donovan.

Robin fitted the cuffs to her hands and headed for the street leading to her house. More than ever she thanked God that Gram lived close enough to the bay that her street didn't climb the hills.

Sam carried his shoes over his shoulder as he paced beside her.

"You want to stop and put those on?"

"It's fine." He glanced behind him. "Is it just me, or did that guy creep you out, too?"

"Sam." She shot him a look full of reproach. "He was worried. You heard him. What's wrong with that?"

"I was with you!" After that, Sam was silent for

half a block. Only when they reached the short walk leading to Gram's front door, did he say, "I'm sorry. I guess I'm letting...things...things that shouldn't bother me get to me."

"You think?"

Sam's gaze was steady and serious for the half second he met her eyes. Then he looked down.

"Oh, Sam." She let one crutch lean on her hip as she reached for him. His fingers met hers, and he finally let her see his face again. "He's a nice guy. He's good looking, all that. But he's not—" She'd been about to say, he's not you. She shook herself and gripped the crutch again. "He's not anybody I'm interested in, OK?"

Sam stared at her for a long minute, and started to shut the door. He stopped, pushed it open again, and leaned forward to kiss her mouth, hard, before he left.

☙❧

He watched her swimming. He giggled behind his hand with the joy of her perfection. If he could only save this in a picture forever, keep it always.

But then, he could. He squirmed into a tighter hiding place, so she wouldn't see him, realized she wouldn't have, anyway, and relaxed. She only saw Sam.

Fair enough. He'd make another one of his pictures, right away, before he forgot the vision, and he'd put Sam in it. Show her she couldn't hide from him.

She'd never be able to hide.

9

Sam was nuts. Out of his mind. Crazy. And yet—if Robin hadn't said she didn't much like the other guy, Sam would never have kissed her. He'd have had that much restraint. Shouldn't have kissed her, anyway.

Because what could she think of him after that?

He was half glad he hadn't stuck around to find out. He peeled his uniform shirt over his head and tossed it across the ambulance door.

Bricker came around the back of the car, his face pale.

"What's up?" Sam dragged a pullover around his waist. Playing in the water the day before had left him with a sore throat, but he wouldn't change that, either. Not the time on the beach, and not the kiss. No matter what Robin thought. It was all worth it.

She hadn't smacked him with one of her crutches, at least. Not that he'd given her time, but he hadn't seen any intent of bodily harm in her eyes, for that half second he'd looked into them.

"Sam."

He looked back at Bricker. "Sorry. I'm listening."

"There were some kids up at Wrigley, said some guy in one of your uniforms stopped them, and was talking to them."

Sam frowned at his friend. "And?"

"And nothing." Bricker held his hands out, frustration strong in the tension of his stance. "That was enough. This climate, any adult male talks to a kid he doesn't know, and he's going to get hauled in."

Sam shook his head. "Meaning?"

"Meaning everyone has to go in to give an alibi. And whoever can't clear himself is gonna be doing a lot of explaining."

Something hot and shocking flooded Sam's chest. So this was what it meant to be under suspicion? "When's it happening?"

"Right now." Bricker jerked his chin, and Sam followed him out of the ambulance bay and across the street to the police station.

Detective Macias watched them as they walked in, nodded his thanks. "All I need to know is what you were doing at three forty yesterday afternoon." He slid report pages to each of them.

Sam studied his and wrote. *I was on the beach with Robin Ingram, 2:30 to 4 PM.* He signed his name, handed it to the detective, and waited to be dismissed.

Detective Macias looked up. "She'll corroborate?"

"Yup. I walked her home. We probably got there a little after four-thirty. And Donovan Haggart can vouch for me as well. We talked to him."

"All right." The man nodded approval. "I'll give them both calls."

Robin would be all the alibi Sam needed, but let them get as much proof as they needed to clear him.

Something nagged at Sam's brain, knocking for attention, but when he tried to focus on it, the feeling slid away into a faint unease. Something about Donovan. Something about talking to him? But Sam had nothing to worry about. Donovan wouldn't lie, and Robin knew where he'd been at that time. They would believe her, because she wanted the killer caught as badly as anybody else on the island.

Because she was his target.

෮๛

The weather warmed before the next game. Saturday morning most of the players showed up without jackets or sweaters.

Robin pulled her hair back into a band and made her way to the lineup.

Danny smiled, wiped a hand over his grizzled face, and jerked his head toward Kerry. "He's been waiting for you."

"We're best friends now."

Danny laughed. "Robin, you're everybody's best friend."

A chuckle behind her made her turn. Donovan posed against the net of the backstop, his camera hung slack in his hand. He lifted his chin when he saw her looking.

She smiled but saved her energy for the game rather than walking over to him.

Danny touched her arm. "I'm putting you fourth, all right? Sam coming?"

"Last I heard." Not that she'd spoken to him lately. Not since the kiss. No. In her mind, it was The Kiss, the beginning of everything.

Donovan pushed forward. "Can't I be her runner?"

Danny studied Donovan for a few moments and shrugged. "She's an adult. She can make her own decisions."

"What about the kids?" Robin asked.

"He's not a stranger anymore. I've cleared him."

Danny grinned for half a second before he went on. "If I thought he was intending anything other than helping—well, he wouldn't get past me. You'd better believe I'd protect any one of these kids with my life. I'd kill for one of them."

Donovan nodded, not at all fazed by Danny's vehemence.

Robin, on the other hand, was reeling. She'd never heard Danny threaten to kill a soul, never heard him use that kind of language. What stress did to people…She shook her head, looking around the park for any sign of Sam.

"You're right. We need to get rid of all the people who hurt our kids." Donovan nodded and smiled at Robin. "Looks like I'm your runner today."

And just then, Sam loped onto the field. He wore his usual sloppy pants, a backwards hat, and a sleeveless gray t-shirt.

Robin's heart slammed against her chest, doing its own version of a happy dance that her legs could never join, and making breathing questionable. She tried to calm herself down. By the time Sam reached the backstop, her heart had quieted and let her smile, at least.

He moved past her and grabbed Danny's arm. "Another girl went missing last night."

Robin clasped a hand to her stomach and a crutch clattered to the dirt.

Donovan picked it up and handed it to her.

She took it without looking at him. "Who was it?"

"An eighteen-year-old tourist named Isabel Solis. Her parents just woke up about an hour ago and realized she wasn't in her room. She was sleeping with her older sister, connecting doors, all that, and no one heard a thing."

Danny, looking far too gray for his age, rubbed his hand over his face. "Dear God, when will this end?"

"I can't stay. I'm joining the search." Sam looked back at Robin. "I'm really sorry, babe." Even as he said it, he glanced behind her. "You coming to help us?"

"Sure. Another kid. I mean, yeah, she's legally an adult, but still…" Donovan's voice faded as he straightened. "Yeah. I've got to take my camera home…"

Danny held out his hand toward Donovan. "I'll take it. You come by the office anytime and pick it up. Just call my cell, and I'll meet you there." He took the camera and glanced at Sam. "Once I get all the team taken care of, send everyone home, I'll join you guys."

Sam nodded and looked at Donovan.

"Yeah. Yeah, sure. OK, let's go." Looking dazed, Donovan followed Sam from the park.

Three other runners went with them.

Robin let go of one crutch to be able to grip Danny's arm. "I'm glad you're cancelling the game."

Danny bowed his head. "I have to, don't I? But I'm not sure the kids will understand."

"Of course they will." Robin moved among the players and their parents, giving the news. Four weeks, seven kidnappings, two deaths. And two children, the most vulnerable of the victims, among the missing. Like Danny, she had to demand of God when it would end.

She didn't hear an answer.

&oc&

Kerry's mother called the meeting, and most of the

team, parents and runners along with the members, showed up. It made for a really crowded front room to her house, but no one wanted to chance meeting outside, where one of the kids could go missing.

Sam had jammed folding chairs into every available space, and kids sat on laps and on the floor.

Kerry shoved onto the couch next to Robin. "Where's Donovan?"

His mother slapped her forehead. "I never called him. He's not on the roster."

Danny patted her hand. "He's really not on the team, remember? He's not even a runner."

"I forgot." Kerry frowned, his face crinkling with his concentration. "I forgot. He's always there, so I forgot."

"That's OK, Kerry." Robin put her arm around him, half to comfort him, and half to give herself a little breathing room.

"The question is, are we going to continue the games until this guy is caught?" Danny looked around the room.

Robin followed his gaze. Concerned parents, anxious kids, team members she'd come to love, all stared at Danny.

"We keep a good eye on everyone," she said. "And everyone has a runner. It's not like we're letting the kids wander off by themselves."

One of the fathers spoke up. "But none of the kids who've gone missing have been alone. Look at that last girl. Isabel. She was in a hotel room, for heaven's sake. How did he get her out without security or her parents or her sister hearing something?"

"I don't know. Maybe she went out on her own. She's a teenager, sometimes they do stuff like that. But our kids need an outlet." Robin needed it. She needed to see these kids, to hold them dear in her heart, to be able to ascertain for herself every week that they were all OK. All protected. Didn't anyone else feel that way? "I just don't think isolating ourselves will keep anyone safe. I think it'll have the opposite effect."

Danny nodded. "You're right there. Maybe we should vote on it. Because if you all want to continue, I'm all for that. But before we do"—he raised his hand over the sound of voices—"We need to pray about it." He bowed his head and waited for silence.

Only one family voted against continuing. The father who had been against it shook his head, gathered his daughter, and left.

"That's fine. That's his decision. I won't blame anyone who chooses to keep their kid home." Danny held out his hands, reassuring. "But I'm not going to take that decision away from anyone who wants to play. I think they'll be back. He's scared. He has a right to be. We all should be. And we each deal with it in a different way."

"She better come back," Kerry said. "We can't be a team without her."

"Sure we can, Kerry." Robin squeezed his shoulder. "We'll miss her, but we're still a team."

Kerry looked around the room. Once again, anxious faces turned toward him, and when he finally nodded, the relief was tangible. "OK, yeah, she's one of us, but it's OK if she can't come. I'll pretend she's got a cold."

After the relieved laughter faded, Mrs. Wright organized handing out the snacks and drinks everyone contributed.

Danny leaned over the back of the couch. "I'm

glad you all decided to stick with the team." He nodded at several parents. "I believe it's the best course. But we have to protect our kids, regardless." He straightened, raised his hand, and using his coach's voice, addressed the team. "Kids, remember, you're safe with the team, or with your parents. No one else. Got that? There's a killer out there, and we don't know who it is. If you ever think you're in danger, you can come to me. Call me. I'd defend any one of you with my life."

Robin's eyes teared up as the others chimed in. Her kids—these kids—at least, would be safe.

The atmosphere charged up to almost a party.

Sam, on the floor across the room, lifted a plastic glass of soda to Robin in a toast. She grinned and returned the gesture. She needed these people so much. *Thank You, God, for not taking them away from me.*

Lillian, mother of a little girl with developmental disabilities, perched on the arm of the couch next to Robin. "I was in your shop the other day. As soon as I said I knew you, Grace showed me all your mermaids. You're very artistic."

"You're autistic?" Kerry, wide-eyed and sad, stared at her. "And you have bad legs, too? I'm sorry. Poor Robin. I'm glad I'm me. Kerry."

Robin shared a grin with Lillian. "I'm glad you're Kerry, too."

He hugged her hard, laughing. "We're both glad I'm Kerry!"

Sam made his way between a pair of twins from the team. "If I say I'm glad you're Kerry, do I get a hug, too?"

Kerry bounced on the couch, nearly tipping Robin into his side. "Are you glad I'm Kerry?"

"I'm *very* glad you're Kerry."

Laughing harder, bent almost double in his glee, Kerry said, "I'm very glad I'm Kerry, too."

"So where's my hug?"

Kerry held out his hands so Sam could pull him to his feet and wrapped his arms around Sam's waist.

Robin met his gaze over Kerry's tousled head. He was such a true friend. Such a true man, a good man. Even if he never fell in love with her, she would never want him out of her life. She treasured what he gave to her too much to throw it away on a whim.

❧◈❧

Sam spent the next morning helping to search the hills directly above Avalon, just beyond the Catalina Island Golf Course. He coughed his way through four hours of scrabbling over rocks, avoiding cactus, and coordinating with the others on the search. They found no sign of any of the missing people, and only succeeded in disturbing the local fauna.

Detective Macias looked up as Sam dragged into the police station.

"Nothing." Sam threw his reflective vest onto the counter and leaned on his elbows, running his hands through his hair. "I even found a cave and thought there might be something in it."

The detective leaned back in his chair, creaking the struts. "Yeah?"

"But it was only about three feet deep. Lots of broken soapstone and no sign of anyone ever having been in it." His voice gave out on the last words, and he coughed until it came back, however rough.

"We're going to find them." Macias narrowed his

eyes.

"I know." Despite how positive he wanted to sound, Sam shook his head. "I know, I'm just afraid it won't be until after they're all dead."

"That's why we're searching."

Sam didn't bother to answer. He pushed away from the counter and rubbed his sunburned face, coughing again. "Makes you wonder what kind of kicks he's getting out of these little scenes he sets up. What is it about Robin that makes him do that?"

"Obviously, he's nuts. Killing grown women." Macias paused, and his voice deepened to heavy significance. "Doing who knows what to the kids he keeps."

Turning away, Sam waved his hand. "Yeah, well, you know as well as anyone else here that we're not looking for a pedophile."

Though the detective didn't move, something in his face hardened, became almost satisfied in anger. "I know it, sure. How do you?"

Sam closed his eyes, berating himself for the slip. "Bricker told me."

"Right. Have a seat." Macias reached for the phone.

Sam sank into the hard chair, knowing that, though Macias looked and sounded almost as calm as ever, Sam had just made himself a suspect. Again, fire shocked his chest, and he could barely keep his hands and feet still. Hearing the other man's muttered questions, though he didn't catch all the words, didn't help.

Ten minutes later Macias hung up and stared at Sam. "Bricker says he would never have told you privileged information. Listen, Albrecht, I need to know how you found this out. I need to know how you knew where to find that baby. Bricker swears the teams went through that warehouse twice before, and you knew it. You were in on those searches. And you still insisted you had to go back. Was that because you'd just put the kid there and wanted to be the hero getting her out?"

"No—"

"You'd better tell me now, Albrecht. Because if you don't have a good explanation, you're not walking out of this station, not unless you plan to lead us to where you've got these people hidden."

Sam leaped to his feet. "Bricker told me! How else would I know he knew? Come on. Robin is my best friend. I've spent the last month helping to search—"

"So has every other able-bodied male in town."

Panic twisted Sam's chest and squeezed. What possessed him to forget he wasn't supposed to know privileged information?

He gripped the edge of Macias' desk, leaning forward and putting all his weight onto his arms and into his words. "I am not the murderer. I am doing everything I can to help find this guy, and you'd rather blame me than look somewhere else."

The phone rang and Macias picked it up, listened a minute, and stood. "Sargent Klou!"

An officer Sam recognized but hadn't talked to much strode into the room. "Sir?"

Macias motioned to Sam. "Take him into custody. But we're not going to process him just yet. We're going to another murder scene." He narrowed his eyes at Sam. "I want to see your face when your audience gets its first look at this new little tableau of yours."

10

Becca kneeled on her mattress and stared at Mr. Bird. Ever since he'd brought Jake to stay, he'd been so mad with her. It made her want to cry and made her mad right back, sometimes. Mad at Jake, but mostly mad at Mr. Bird, because he didn't have to bring Jake here. He'd just ruined everything, making Jake stay when he didn't even like Jake, and Jake didn't like him, and everybody being mad all the time.

Besides, he never said Jake was gonna help him with his story, and if he wasn't, then why was he there? He just made everything bad.

But now Mr. Bird smiled and gave Becca a brown paper sack. He gave one to Jake, too.

She opened hers and grinned. Not another sandwich, instead, she found milk and cookies, and a chocolate bar underneath.

"This is dinner?" Jake asked.

Becca flinched, sure Mr. Bird would smack Jake for being snotty again.

"More or less." Mr. Bird squatted on the mattress next to Becca. "Eat up, honey. I'm going to tell you a story."

Jake snorted, but he was too busy eating to say anything to make Mr. Bird mad.

Feeling like her daddy had suddenly come back and wrapped her in his safe arms, Becca snuggled next to Mr. Bird. "I like stories."

"This one is about my little robin bird."

Becca pulled away to look into Mr. Bird's face. "Is this the story I'm going to help you with?"

Mr. Bird smiled. "Yes, it is. You're going to help me tell the whole world about my little robin, and how I fixed her. She's such a good bird, but she was so sad, because she couldn't walk right. There was something wrong with her legs. No one cared. They just let her try to hop around without trying to make her legs better." Mr. Bird stroked Becca's shoulder. "I was the only person who cared. So what I did was to make her legs all better. I had to use special magic to do it, but as soon as I was done, she could walk, and she could run, and climb. We climbed across the beach and the rocks and played in the waves and swam around the bay. And when she got tired, we went into a special little place where it was quiet, and we took a nap." He smiled. "We're still there."

Jake said, "Huh."

Mr. Bird blinked like he was just waking up. "What?"

"You're not there. You're here."

He muttered something about crazy people, and Becca tried to pull her shoulders as close to her chest as she could.

"You don't understand," Mr. Bird said. "It's all magic, you know. I'm there, but no one can see me." He ran one finger across his upper lip. "Your scout leader helped me a lot with it. He helped me stay invisible. I owe him a lot."

"You mean Simon is OK?"

"Sure, he's OK. Why wouldn't he be?"

Instead of acting happy, Jake stared at Mr. Bird for

a long time and turned away, wiping his face.

Becca thought he was crying.

She tipped her head back again to look at Mr. Bird. "Robin's the best little bird in the whole wide world, isn't she?"

"She sure is." Mr. Bird stood up. "I'll bring your dinner later."

But he never came back, and Becca fell asleep still tasting chocolate in her mouth.

∂∞∂

Because of the tide coming in, the police and their captive had to hurry across the same beach Sam and Robin played on a few days before, and around the promontory. They skirted a cliff that jutted into the sea and climbed over a jumble of rocks. They'd get soaked on the way back. How the police would protect the crime scene and get all the information they needed, Sam couldn't imagine. Macias hadn't put him in cuffs, and Sam thanked God for that, but having to follow the detective, and having Sergeant Klou dog his heels made him want to punch someone.

Cuffs might have been a better move on their part.

Foam curled past his wet sneakers and he moved farther up the beach.

Detective Macias grabbed his arm. "Not yet." He motioned to the sergeant, and Klou angled himself ahead, going round a bend so Sam could see only the top of his head.

Three other officers gathered around what Sam knew would be a grisly, staged figure.

Another dead girl, and he was being forced to look at her body. He still had to fight down the images of

Lehanie that wandered through his dreams. He didn't need this.

Robin would be worried about nightmares and this time, she'd have reason. *God, help us to find the killer.* He'd prayed this a million times and was sure God was answering. Just not on Sam's timetable.

The detective jerked his head for Sam to follow.

One thing about the monster, he loved beauty. The couple—because there were two—Simon Carson, the missing scout leader and the newly-missing Isabel Solis—were beautifully posed. Wire and twine did their ghoulish magic, held the two in a position that should have looked stilted, and yet seemed natural.

Isabel's hair had been dyed black, of course, and blue irises painted on her eyelids. The man's hair had been dyed as well, a rusty sort of brown that matched Sam's. The killer had foregone the crutches this time. Isabel lay across Simon's arms, one arm around his neck, the other flung out as though she were inviting the tide in to take them out to sea forever.

The beautiful, sickening sight made Sam's stomach clench. "Two," he mumbled.

Macias glanced at him. Sam felt his jerk as he turned. "What's that?"

"There's two of them. He's not happy with just one at a time. He has to go after two. I guess that's what he wanted with the scouts." Anger rose up, filled his chest. He wanted to smash something, crush it with his bare hands, and wasn't surprised to realize he wanted to do all that to the killer's throat.

"Yeah, well, who do they remind you of?" No one could mistake the sneer in Macias's voice.

"Robin and me. But you have to know I didn't do that. I would never—" He stopped. Protests would convince nobody. "Look, this had to have happened in the last eight hours or so. I've spent the last four searching."

Macias planted one foot on a rock and pulled out his memo pad. "And before that?"

Sam slumped. "I was asleep. Eating breakfast. Getting ready to join the search." And searching alone most of that time, which meant not much of an alibi.

"Not arranging your gruesome little tableau?" Macias shot a glance at Klou and back at Sam.

"No. That wasn't me." Sam ran his hand through his hair. "But I'll tell you what. I carried Robin down to the water a few days ago. Donovan saw us. I told you that. The killer could have seen us, as well."

"Right. You trying to set Haggart up for this?"

Sam heard the triumph in the man's voice. "No, of course not." But a part of him jumped to claim that answer. Better than the police suspecting him of wanting to hurt Robin.

"He's got alibis. Keeps a notebook, I gather. He's very organized. He was either at the shop where Robin works, or with Kerry. In fact, that day he saved Kerry's life was one of the worst. It was the day the boy and his scout leader went missing, remember?"

"He didn't necessarily save Kerry's life—"

"What is with you, Albrecht? Kerry doesn't mean anything to you? I thought you were pretending to be his best friend. Of course, I could say the same thing about you and Robin."

"I am not stalking her. I am not kidnapping children. I am not a murderer."

Klou stepped between them.

Waves lapped their feet, coming close to the bodies. The cliffs rose behind them, and only a strip of sand still sat above the water level. "We've got to move them."

Detective Macias slapped his notebook shut. "You got everything you need?"

Klou nodded.

"Get them out."

⚜

Now, when he got confused, he could look at the pictures from the beach. They gave him purpose again. Her hair, her eyes, so very blue, he could stare into them forever. Someday, she'd have to let him.

He opened his photo viewer and scrolled through to his favorite picture. She looked so peaceful, like an angel had come to her and blessed her with peace. And she didn't know anything about him—yet.

She'd look even happier when she knew.

⚜

"They've found another couple of bodies," Grace said. "That tourist girl and the scout leader. The two kids still haven't shown up."

Robin jerked her head so her cell phone nearly went flying and pulled it back so she could answer Grace, who sounded much too thrilled. "When did you hear?" But she knew. Grace's cousin had a police scanner. She'd probably heard the gossip before Sam, as an ambulance driver, knew he had more bodies to pick up. "I have to go. I have to call Sam."

"You do that. And let me know what he says, all right? He can give us some real insider info."

Robin shuddered as she shut her cell. She could

half understand Grace's fascination, but really, even if she didn't expect at least one of those bodies to have black hair and blue painted eyes, she'd find it all repulsive.

Sam's phone rang five times before she was directed to leave a message. "I suppose you're at work, or maybe out of range, searching. They found two of the missing people, Grace told me." And she couldn't think how to end the message. *Hurry to me, because I need you? I need to know you're all right?* Instead, she pressed END and tucked her phone into her pocket. She shifted her crutches once again and headed home for a shower. The game was just a few hours away. If Sam was at work, she wasn't sure she wanted to play, but the team had dwindled so much in the last few weeks that she might not have a choice.

God, please, bring this to an end. I don't think I can stand much more.

❧❧

They had to understand now. How could they look at his art, the best he'd done so far, and not see it? Not see Robin free of her crutches now, free to dance and play the way she was meant to, and not make the connection?

Still, he had plenty of story left to tell them.

The wedding.

Maybe a honeymoon. Perfect place to have one, on Catalina Island. The thought made him laugh.

Then the children. A boy and a girl, the perfect family. It would be nice to have that baby for the last one. Still, if he wanted to, he could find another one. Easy. If he wanted to.

He'd probably want to.

He could see it in his head already, as clear as he'd seen all the other pictures. Robin holding an infant, the little girl leaned against her knee, and that knee had no brace on it. The boy would be looking at his dad—at him—with that adoring look kids got when they were with their dads. He wouldn't have to dye Robin's hair or paint her eyes. She'd be perfect. The whole scene would be perfect.

He'd have to use the timer delay so he could put himself into the picture. They'd see, finally, when they looked through his portfolio, the careful attention he paid to every sweet detail, see his genius, read his story and understand.

❧❧

In all the time he had worked for the county, Sam had never seen the inside of the jail from this perspective—that of criminal. He submitted his fingerprints to file, although they already had them, and his body to indignity, and his clothing for a jumpsuit. He tried to call Robin, got her grandmother, and asked her to set up a lawyer for him. He wanted to ask for prayers, as well. Nothing short of the Divine would help now, not after his mistakes.

The contempt of the people now in charge of his life stung. The fact that he was no longer considered a citizen of the world, but rather, a despoiler, an enemy, a *murderer*, stung. Worse than that, the knowledge that Robin would have to learn about this, destroyed him.

He sat on the edge of the metal bunk in the empty cell and held his head in his hands. He wasn't guilty. He hadn't kidnapped or killed a soul. Somehow, the accusations made him question his sanity, his truth. And if he, the only person other than the killer who knew that truth, doubted, what did that mean for every other person who knew him?

Robin.

What did it mean for Robin?

He pictured her on the beach, the last time he'd really seen her smile. He pictured her face dewed with ocean water, her hair damp and tangled. He felt again her body in his arms and his shoulders began to shake.

He did not want her faith in him destroyed, and yet, what choice would she have?

And the only prayer he could come up with was, *Oh, God, oh, God, oh, God...*

Even then, he wasn't sure God heard.

❦

Robin dressed as quickly as she could and tied her hair back. What she ought to do was dye it blonde. Bleach it, rather, since hair as black as hers needed the strongest chemicals to change its color. If she did that, what would the monster do? Leave off stalking her? Leave off the kids? Start buying a different color hair dye?

She slumped on the edge of her bed. She didn't know how she knew, but nothing would make him stop, nothing short of being caught.

Maybe she ought to put herself out there where he could catch her. And she'd catch him in return, right? Why hadn't anyone thought of that already? Dangle her out like bait and let him go after her, and they'd have him.

Who would do this? Robin couldn't believe it of

anyone. The scenes she'd read about or had heard described weren't anything she could relate to reality. She couldn't picture anyone she knew, couldn't picture some sinister stranger, staging stiff bodies, playing his disturbing dress up games with them. Whoever had done that must be pure evil.

Couldn't picture it and didn't want to. When she thought of the murderer, he was a shadowy, inhuman demon, not someone she knew.

She pulled on her uniform and reached for her phone to call Sam again. With her fingers on speed dial, she stopped, and covered her lips with her fingers, remembering the warmth of his mouth over hers. It hadn't been a soft kiss or a gentle one. It had held a world of desperation that she wondered at—was it mostly based on the tension brought on by the murders, or did his feelings actually have something to do with her? And if not, what was the man doing kissing her? Much less, kissing her like *that*.

But what if he meant it? What if all the longing and dread Robin had felt in him had to do more with his feelings for her, his worry for her, because he cared—as more than just a friend?

She couldn't go there, didn't want to, and yet a part of her, much too large a part to be dismissed and shoved away into her subconscious—believed it. And as much as she didn't want to start to count on it, she wanted to believe with every cell in her body that he loved her.

Love did such crazy things to people.

"The bus is here." Grams stopped at her door and looked in. "Are you all right, kiddo? You sure you don't want to sit this one out?" Worry lined her forehead, and her hands twisted together.

Robin raised her chin. "No. I have to be there for the team." Even though she'd much rather shut the door on the outside world and live in her imagination for a few days. She could put it to good use and make more dolls. She'd slacked off on sewing the last week or so.

Grams couldn't read her mind, and so she helped Robin to her feet, helped her fit her crutches to her arms. Robin didn't need the help, not really, but she needed the comfort. Grams was good that way.

Robin straggled out to the bus and waited for the lift to carry her to the top step. Once inside, she clumped to the first open seat. Only two other teammates were there, along with one family member. There should have been more. The driver never varied his route, and he should have already picked up Kerry.

Robin fingered her cell in her pocket and debated calling Kerry's mother. Kerry might just be sick. He might have pulled a muscle. He might have told his mom he was too scared to go to the game. That wasn't likely, though.

She decided not to call. At the moment, she didn't want to know.

Halfway to the park, the driver answered a call and pulled to the side. He looked around, his voice bland. "Due to unforeseen circumstances, the game has been canceled." The expression in his eyes didn't match his voice, and Robin's shoulders tensed.

They'd only picked up six players so far. Robin pulled herself to her feet and thumped toward the front of the bus. "What happened?"

The driver shook his head. "Danny didn't say. Just canceled the game and told me to take everyone home. Said to make sure all the kids get right inside before I leave each house."

Robin sank into an empty seat and bowed her head. *Oh, God, not more kidnappings. Please don't let anyone else have gone missing. Please stop this person from hurting any more children, much less killing more adults.*

She leaned forward. "Can you arrange to let me off last? I want to make sure—" She choked. "Make sure, too, OK?"

"That's all right." The driver glanced over his shoulder as he pulled back onto the street and passed a golf cart. "I know just how you feel."

They'd dropped the twins and their mother off when Robin's cell chirped. She dug it out of her pocket and checked the number. Grams.

"What's up?"

"You coming home?"

"How'd you know?" Robin had to cover her free ear to hear.

"Danny called." Grams paused. "Oh, kiddo. You're not gonna like this."

"Grams?" Robin's throat tightened, and she could barely say the name.

"Honey, I hate to tell you this, but Sam called, too. He wanted to—he said he wanted you to hear it from me. And you needed to know right away. They're charging Sam."

The world ended. Disappeared. All that was left was a void that had swallowed her whole, without warning. "What?"

"I called a lawyer for him. Poor Sam, he sounds like he's already convicted and headed for the chair. Sure didn't sound very hopeful. Apparently, he knew about some bit of evidence that he shouldn't have."

Robin tried to swallow. She couldn't. "Why would

that make them—"

Grams overrode her protests. "Robin, I hate to say this, but from the things he said, it sounds like that Macias man thinks it's been Sam all along."

11

It was *not* Sam.

Everything Robin knew, everything she believed, everything she loved, the very core of her being knew that to be true. It wasn't Sam.

But if they'd arrested him, that meant they weren't looking for anyone else, and that meant the island citizens were at risk. All they had to do, she thought with bitter irony, was to wait for another kidnapping, or another twisted, dressed-up body to turn up. That'd show 'em. Robin shook her head. She wanted Sam proved innocent but not at the expense of yet another life. They'd lost too many already. Now she was holed up in her room, just like she'd wanted to be, and she didn't like it.

But there had been reporters outside the house when she'd come home, already, and they made it clear they weren't going to leave her alone.

So far, she hadn't talked to any of them. What could she say? That she believed Sam innocent, so they, and the police, could start looking at her for complicity? After all, these grisly murders didn't have to be a threat to her at all.

Maybe that Detective Macias had already come to the same conclusion—decided that Robin was in on it all with Sam, that the two of them had made a pact to decorate the island with scenes from some morbid fantasy they'd cooked up together. Maybe the cops were just waiting for her to make the wrong move and prove them right.

And how could she save Sam when she was so scared?

She had to make some sort of statement. She had to put together the words that would do the most good, help the police to find the killer—the real killer. But how could she know what those words were when she didn't know who they would be directed toward? If she knew who the killer was, she might have a better idea of how to lure him into the open.

She bent over her clasped hands for a few moments, speechless, so conflicted that her thoughts trembled and crashed against each other and made no sense. She struggled to bring some sort of order to her prayer.

God, I need help. I don't want to blame someone who might be innocent, but the police have already done that, and I need to help Sam. I need him! Give me the right words, please. Help me to help Sam. And to help the ones who are still missing. Especially Becca and Jake. Those two are only children. Oh, God!

There it was, a prayer full of need. Begging for favors. No praise, no thanksgiving, nothing but need. Thank God, He understood.

Anguish held her motionless for what seemed like hours, and when she finally shifted, her back and legs had become so stiff it hurt to move.

She scooted her desk chair closer to her computer and tapped the keys for a few minutes. Pretty soon she'd open that front door, face the reporters, and give her statement.

"I'm appalled. You can't imagine the depth of my feelings. The island has been struggling with the death of its citizens for weeks, and now that they have Sam behind bars—"

She paused, reread the paragraph and shook her head. Erased "Sam behind bars." Added, "...now they have arrested Sam, I'm sure things will change."

She read it over again and again. She needed to memorize it, and she wanted it to be as ambiguous as possible, without sounding as though she'd intended that. People hearing or reading it would think, of course, that she believed Sam guilty. She would know she didn't. If Sam heard about her statement, she hoped he'd know what she really meant, too.

Because as soon as her words went live, she'd do what she'd been thinking of for the last few days. Put herself out there. Give the killer a chance at her. Maybe he didn't want it, but she wouldn't know until she tried, would she?

She didn't have any other choice.

❧

Ever since Mr. Bird yelled at them, and Jake started crying about his friend, even though Mr. Bird promised his friend was OK, Becca knew she was in trouble. And it wasn't because of the hole in the wall.

It was because Jake was right. He'd been right the whole time, ever since Mr. Bird shoved him in the room from behind. He was right about Mr. Bird. Mr. Bird wasn't as nice as he'd pretended. Jake said Mr. Bird lied. He lied sometimes about bringing them food, or taking out the trash, or cleaning the toilet in the bathroom. So he probably lied about Jake's friend, too.

Mr. Bird wasn't nice at all.

And that meant her mommy and daddy didn't

know where she was. If they did, they would have come to get her. They wouldn't like Mr. Bird to keep her away from them.

Mr. Bird lied and Becca didn't like him anymore.

Jake, face down on the other mattress, sniffed. "My scout leader was the best guy in the world. He taught me how to start a fire, and when my dad got sick, he let me hang around all the time. Like a brother or something. Now I'm never gonna see him again."

Becca crawled next to Jake. She put her hand on his back, and he didn't push her away. She rubbed his shoulder, and he let her.

"If we pray, God will take care of us."

Jake sat up. He rubbed a fist over one eye. "I hate him."

"Who? God?" Becca nearly fell backward off the mattress.

"No. That Mr. Bird. I hate him. I hope God kills him right now. If I had a gun I'd shoot him."

"That's bad." Becca tried not to sound like a baby, but she probably did anyway. "God doesn't want anyone to kill anyone else."

"Yeah, well, Mr. Bird sure doesn't listen."

Becca chewed on her lip for a minute. "Sometimes, I don't listen."

Jake snorted and wiped his nose on his sleeve. "What? You go around killing people?"

"No. But sometimes I'm bad." She peered up from under her lashes. "Real bad."

Jake shrugged and lay down again. "So what? It's not like anyone cares."

"God cares." Becca kneeled on the cement floor. "I promised I'd be good, and I wasn't. I been real bad. I made a hole in the wall."

"What?" Jake rolled back again. "Here? You made a hole in the wall *here*?"

Becca nodded. "Next to my mattress."

"OK, this I gotta see." Jake crawled to her side of the room. "Show it to me."

At least, he'd stopped crying.

She kneeled next to her mattress and shoved the pillow away from the wall. Jake pulled at the edge of the mattress, and when that didn't show him everything, he tugged the other side until he could see all the way down to the floor. But his excitement disappeared like a popped balloon. "That's not a hole. It doesn't even go all the way through."

"But I dug it, and it was bad."

Jake poked at it. "How'd you do it?"

"With my nails. 'Member how Mr. Bird always complains 'cuz my nails look bad? It's 'cuz I dig." She hung her head. "I can't help it. I ask God to make me behave, but He doesn't. I just keep digging."

Jake glanced over his shoulder at the door and lay on her mattress with his face close to the hole. "Was there anything there when you first got here? I mean, did you dig this whole thing yourself?" He looked back at her. "There wasn't already a little hole in the paint or something?"

"No. I did it." Becca stuck her thumb in her mouth even though Jake didn't act mad.

"We could make it bigger," he said. He sat up and frowned. "But we need something stronger than just fingernails."

"Why?"

He looked at her, still frowning. "To make it bigger."

"Uhn-uh! If it gets any bigger, Mr. Bird will see it."

"No, that's OK. We'll crumple up the sheets over it, and keep your pillow folded over it, too. I'll help." He turned and grabbed Becca's shoulders. "We can't let him see it, but we gotta make it bigger. Maybe we can make it go all the way outside, and we can crawl through. Or we can yell and someone will hear us and come get us."

"Really?"

"Yeah. Really. I just don't know what we can use."

Becca looked around. The only toys were a couple of stuffed animals, a bear and a bunny. The bunny scared her, because it had a creepy, way-too-big smile sewn across its face. But even a creepy stuffed toy wouldn't be any good for digging. "Can you dig with books?" She got one of the picture books Mr. Bird had left.

Jake grimaced. "I dunno. We can try." He tried to use the corner of the book, but it just bent the cardboard back. After a few minutes he threw it down. "That's not gonna work."

He got up and looked around the room. "There's nothing else here. Not even curtains or curtain rods." He put his hands on his hips and turned in a slow circle. "Hey, are there any little metal cars?"

"My brother has lots, but Mr. Bird doesn't have any." Nothing but a couple mattresses, some pillows, some sheets, the nasty yellow light way up out of their reach, the two toys and some books.

And two kids.

"This is what we're gonna do. We're gonna take turns. If we work all the time, instead of only when you're supposed to be going to sleep, it'll get bigger a lot faster."

"I don't know if we should." Becca hunched her

shoulders, thinking of how Mr. Bird would yell if he found that hole. Yell, and maybe do something worse.

"No, it'll be OK. I'll take a turn right now. You sit near the door, and if you hear Mr. Bird coming, you tell me, and I'll get up and put everything in front of it, to hide it, real quick, then run. He might check to see what I'm doing if he sees me on your bed. And when I get tired, you can dig. And we'll just keep digging as long as we can."

Becca wrapped shaky arms around her middle. "But it's bad!"

"No, it isn't." Jake squatted in front of her. "It's not bad, Becca. It's OK. I promise. At home, it'd be bad, but here, it's good. Cuz we need to get out." He stood and lay back down on her mattress. "Go listen, OK? And Becca?"

Becca sat next to the door, her heart hammering. "What?"

"I think God didn't make you stop because He *wanted* you to make a hole in the wall."

❧❦

They wouldn't let Robin see Sam or talk to him. *Conflict of interest*, Detective Macias kept saying, but she had no idea how that would work. Sam was her friend and accused of murder, and she wanted to see him and didn't plan to break Sam out with smuggled nail files.

No, she'd get him out by finding the real killer. Because who had the killer proved he was after with every crime scene he laid out for them to find?

Robin.

Bait. She'd be bait.

She wasn't about to share that with Detective Macias, though. Nasty man. She glared at his face on the TV as he talked about how they planned to come up with more substantial evidence by the time Sam went to trial. They wouldn't. How could they? Evidence against an innocent man?

No. Long before that, they'd have the real killer handed to them. By Robin. By limpy, gimpy little Robin. Because really, that kiss hadn't been long enough, and she needed to get Sam out and kissing her again so she could make sure he really meant what she thought he meant. What she hoped he meant.

Her cell rang, and she answered without checking the number sure it would be Sam, sure he'd been released, cleared. She heard Detective Macias's voice, and her heart sank.

"Albrecht ever make you feel threatened?"

"No, of course not."

"Uneasy? The way he looks at you? Touches you? Talks to you?"

"No." She felt her defenses rise up against this officer who wanted to frame the man she loved. He made her feel childish and anxious at the same time.

"That day on the beach, when he used you as an alibi—"

"He was there. I told you that."

"I understand." He didn't say he believed either one of them. "Anything he did that day that made you feel uncomfortable?"

"He didn't, no."

Detective Macias went on. "The kids on your team. I know he's close to some of them. That doesn't bother you?"

"No, and it doesn't bother them, either. It

shouldn't. He's fine. He loves them. He'd die to protect them." Only when she took a breath did she realize she'd echoed Danny's claim.

"How about the way he talks about the victims?"

"He's angry. Sad. All the normal feelings any human would have in this situation."

"I see." She heard papers rustle before he said, "How about when he talks about other people? He got any suspicions?"

"He says the person who's doing this is nuts."

Macias's tone strengthened. "Look, Robin, I know you're not happy, but you've got to tell me anything that will help. You don't want anything to happen to the two kids who are still missing, do you?"

As if it would be her fault if she didn't offer up a suspect. Should she tell him her idea? See what he thought of using her as bait?

"Why are you asking me? I don't *know* who this is. Do you think I'm protecting someone?"

"If you were, it would be Sam, wouldn't it?"

Robin ran a shaking hand through her hair. What would it take to convince this guy that Sam had nothing to do with the murders? Besides another murder when he was in jail.

Macias cleared his throat. "Thank you for your time, Ms. Ingram. If you think of anything else that could help us, don't hesitate to call me. You have my cell number."

Fuming, Robin got out her golf cart, which she'd remembered to plug in the night before, and drove it down to the co-op. How could the detective live with himself, knowing he'd thrown an innocent man in jail and left the rest of the world prey to a killer?

Someone was the killer, and it wasn't Sam. And

Robin could still do her part to draw the killer out. It had to be someone she'd recognize.

Someone who would recognize her.

Who would take the bait?

He wouldn't have agreed to her scheme, she was sure of that. Fair enough. She'd do it all on her own.

She took a deep breath, climbed from her cart, and crutched her way to the co-op's open door.

And who best to spread the news than Grace? Grace, who seemed to talk to every citizen on the island on at least a weekly basis, knew all the news, and passed it on as well. She'd always felt guilty about being a part of the gossip, but if it helped Sam—

She stood with her head bowed for a moment, begged for guidance, gripped her crutches and her courage, and stepped through the door.

Donovan looked up from the counter. "Hey, Robin, how you doing? These fine people have been checking out your mermaids." He turned to the kids gathered in front of the display. "This is the lady who sews those dolls. Makes up the design and everything."

She'd never told him that. That had probably been Grace. It was the sort of thing Grace would do to make Robin seem more attractive in the eyes of an eligible male.

"Mom's gonna buy us each one," the taller of the two girls said.

Robin smiled. "Thanks." But she couldn't quite keep her mind on any possible profits. Once she'd decided that it was up to her to bring the killer out in the open—after her—she couldn't concentrate on anything to do with the rest of her future.

She might not have one.

She'd do everything she could to make sure she did. The most important part was to clear Sam, get him out of jail, and find out if he loved her. She had to stay alive for that, didn't she? Stay alive for another kiss?

If she just kept her focus on that kiss, maybe she could fool the killer into thinking she didn't suspect a thing.

The mother paid for their purchases and the family left. A few other customers roamed the aisles but not within hearing distance.

Robin leaned forward so her crutches supported more of her weight.

"Isn't Grace supposed to be in today?"

"She was, yeah." Donovan came around the counter to put away a few things the family had decided against. "I gather her husband has the flu, so she's home taking care of him and keeping her germs from spreading."

"Nice of her." Robin sighed. So much for spreading her own news. She could tell Donovan, but then, he probably wouldn't be as quick to spread it as Grace. Besides that, he'd probably try to talk her out of it. Sam would.

She sighed again. "You heard about Sam?"

Donovan glanced at her. "Yeah. Shock, that."

"Can I sit down?" She edged around to the back of the counter, and Donovan stepped back to let her pass.

"Thanks. Some days I just can't manage, you know?"

"That's too bad. Why don't you do something about it?"

"Something? Like what?"

As he watched her, she looked back at him, considering. He liked her. Grace insisted he did. And she needed help.

He avoided looking at her legs. "Surgery. Get your legs fixed. They can do that, can't they?"

So she needed fixing, did she? She stood, anger burning away the need. "I had eight surgeries between the time I was four and the time I was six," she said through gritted teeth. "If I hadn't, I wouldn't be able to walk as well as I can now. But they did as much as they could."

"You mean this is it? You're not going to get any better?"

"No. I'm not." She stared into his eyes. She was not going to react any further to his attitude. She was just fine the way she was, thank you, and she didn't need to be *fixed*. At least Sam liked her as she was, gimpy legs and all. Robin liked herself just as she was, as well. And since she knew for a fact that God loved her, no matter what, that made it unanimous.

Donovan's opinion didn't count.

But if she just looked at his attitude, and not what she needed for Sam, how much good would she do for her best friend? She took a deep breath, let go of her resentment, and unclenched her jaw. "I'm just having a really hard time processing everything that's happened. All the murders and Sam's arrest." She had to get him talking, and her legs weren't on her list of approved subjects.

Donovan nodded, his brows slightly furrowed. "He seemed like an OK guy. Not like someone who'd do something like that."

"Why do you think he did?"

Donovan's eyes widened. "Why are you asking me?"

"Because I can't ask Sam, and I need to get it

straight in my head. I need to understand it."

"Yeah. OK." He shrugged. "I never thought about why he'd do that. I mean, going after girls like that, it's sick. And the boys." He slanted a look at her. "Sorry, I know he's your friend. Or he was. But guys who molest little kids deserve to die."

He was so right.

Slowly, Donovan went on. "You know what most people would do to people like Sam?"

"Donovan, really, I don't need the details."

He blinked as though this was the first time she'd come into focus for him all day. "He made those women look like you."

Robin shuddered at the thought.

He went on. "Do you ever wonder why he did that? Black hair, blue eyes. The crutches." His hand snaked out to stroke her head. "And he had a thing for you."

"Does he?" If only that were true.

"You never saw him watching you. I did."

"I think you're wrong." Robin turned away. "We're friends. That's all. We're *still* friends. I don't care what everyone else thinks of him. He's innocent. He would never hurt anyone like that."

"Oh, Robin." He shook his head. "Look, if you'd like, I'll try to—I don't know. Try to find some proof for you. OK? Would that help?"

"What kind of proof?" she asked, her chin up. "To give the police more reason to blame him?"

"No, no, I didn't mean that at all. No. I meant— you know, to see if we could figure out who really did it."

She nodded, unable to say a word. She needed help as much as she needed protection. Stronger than iron walls, she needed God.

And with God's help, she would expose the monster someone carried around inside him. She had to focus on setting herself out as bait, not on his aberrations. At what risk, she didn't know. Didn't care. She just had to get him to stop.

How? That was the hard part.

Had she really given this enough thought? Probably not. But she was here, and she needed help, and Donovan was the only person she could count on.

"The thing is, now that Sam's—well, gone, I need a runner for the games."

"Are you asking me to step in?"

"Well." She looked at him from under her lashes. "You offered a while back, but since I already had Sam I didn't think I needed another runner."

"But things have changed." Something glinted in his eyes. Now they looked grayer than ice.

"Yeah, things have changed."

"OK. I'm good with that." He shrugged. "I heard Danny canceled the last two games. Are you guys meeting on Saturday?"

"I think so. I'll let you know." Now her heart pounded. She had, at least, a place to start.

"Sounds good." He hesitated. "Look, Robin, if it's not Sam—and believe me, I'm willing to believe it isn't—who do you think it is? Has Sam got any ideas?"

"Not really and neither do I." At least, not any she was willing to tell Donovan about. He could probably play the caveman as easily as Sam.

"OK. Fair enough." He scratched his head. "Look, I've got a few suspicions of my own." And when she opened her mouth to demand he tell her, he held up his hand. "No. I'm going to check a few things out first.

See what I can turn up, you know?"

She hadn't even told him the worst of her plans, and he was taking over. But she struggled to repress her reservations. After all, the more people trying to get Sam out of jail, and out of trouble, the better. She nodded. "OK. Call me when you figure anything out." She didn't make it a request.

"Got it." He smiled, and turned as a new group of customers came inside. "Hi," he called. "Welcome. If you need anything, let me know."

Robin slid off the stool. "Thanks, Donovan. See you later."

He nodded and she made her way to her cart.

This had to be a lot safer than asking the killer to come get her. It might take longer, but Sam was safe, even if he wasn't happy. With Donovan's help, she'd manage all her dreams, alive.

12

But first, she opened her cell and dialed Macias's private number. "You told me if I thought of anything else to call you."

"Right. What have you got for me?"

"I had an idea about how to draw this guy out."

"Draw him out? I'm not sure I understand what you're getting at."

"He wants me, right?"

"Oh, no." At least she'd gotten the man's attention. "Ms. Ingram—"

"Detective Macias, please. Just hear me out. Sam isn't the killer. I know that, even if you refuse to admit it. You asked for my help? Well, I'm going to give it to you. Because obviously the killer is after me, in some twisted, sick way. And I—"

"And you are going to do nothing." From the sound of his voice, Robin thought he'd stood up, maybe was pacing. "You're not going to put yourself in danger. We're looking for evidence on Albrecht. We don't find it, you'll get your boyfriend back. But you are not going to put yourself in danger. If I think you are, I'll have you in custody, as well, for your own safety."

Robin closed her phone and dragged herself back to her cart. Dumb move, she had to admit. Although, maybe she'd gotten the reaction she wanted. Maybe she had really been asking, should I, and Macias had answered, absolutely not.

And so she'd let herself be forced to promise she'd do nothing stupid, nothing dangerous.

What else could she do for Sam? Pray—but she'd been praying all along, and things just seemed to get worse.

The police were looking for evidence to convict Sam.

It wasn't out there. Evidence against someone else—sure. And after what she'd heard about the last murders, how the bodies had been posed on the beach, it had to be someone who had been watching her and Sam that day.

Who else besides Donovan had seen them on the beach? Her shoulders slumped. How could she know? Donovan was the only one who had come up to talk to them, but that didn't mean he alone had seen them. The beach was public, and neither she nor Sam had paid any attention to anyone else that magical afternoon.

If only she'd looked around...

๛๛

Someday, she'd look at him with that same expression she kept for Sam. Someday, *he'd* be her hero.

Maybe he ought to use Sam. Dye his own hair and paint himself up to look like him. That would be a laugh. He was giggling already, thinking it out.

Might make it a little harder to get away with it, but hey, he was good.

He shook his head. Hard. Banged his fist on his temple. Because the whole point was to show them what a genius he was. He didn't want to fall back into obscurity. He wanted them to see—see him, see his vision.

If he had to use Sam, he would, but it was all about him and Robin. Always had been. And that's how it would end up.

∽❧

She ran the cart against the curb and made herself stop her headlong rush to—what? Where was she going? She couldn't even remember now. She stared at the bistro in front of her, at the clear windows that reflected the bay behind her, at the figure of the man who stopped behind her.

She spun around.

"Robin, are you OK? You look—" Donovan smiled, peered closer and stepped forward, his hand out to help her from the cart. "Grace came back and took over so I could come make sure you were all right. You really looked like—I don't know—but bad. Come on. Let's get you some tea or something." He jerked his head at the restaurant behind him.

Robin nodded and scooted off the seat. Without the buzz of the cart's wheels whirring, she caught the sound of the wind, the waves booming on the shore. The sound of normal for the town.

She gripped her crutches and shuffled past Donovan's hand.

He held a chair, asked her what she wanted, and went to the counter to put in the order. When he came back a few minutes later with steaming Styrofoam cups, she'd steeled herself beyond the blank stare of shock and took her drink with a smile.

"Thanks. Don't know what's wrong with me."

He sat, frowning. "Stress, maybe? I mean, you're under a lot. Your boyfriend just got arrested. It's no wonder you're numb."

He certainly understood how she felt. She swallowed, unable to answer.

"I talked to Detective Macias." Donovan shifted his chair, took a drink of his own tea, and pushed a plastic plate loaded with Danish across to her.

Robin cleared her throat. "Right. He told me." She looked up.

Donovan angled his chair so the sun through the windows hit him full in the face, as though the pale November light could bring warmth or color to his skin. "OK, so you know I'm doing whatever I can to clear him. It's up to us, isn't it, you and me? No one else seems interested. Although I gave the detective some info that interested him."

Robin set her cup on the table. "What info?"

"I shouldn't tell you, but—" he grinned. "About Danny Salvator."

"Coach Danny?" Now she straightened, fully engaged. "What on earth could you tell them about the coach?"

"Lots of things. I watch people, Robin. You know how I do. And I see things other people miss." He filled his voice with dark significance, nodding. If he could tell her something she should know—if he could help her help Sam—she had to stay with him. She had to save Sam.

When he remained silent, she moved her hands impatiently. "Tell me."

He slanted her a glance from his ice-colored eyes, toying with her this time, and shook his head. "I can't really, you know." He motioned with his hand, indicating security and secrecy, which irritated her.

She looked away from him, thinking. "When did you tell them this? I mean, tell them whatever it is you've got against Danny?"

"Last night."

So Detective Macias had suspected Danny before Donovan talked to him. Did that mean the kids from the team were in danger? Kerry? She couldn't lose Kerry.

Donovan reached across the table and patted her hand. "Don't worry. And I think Macias is going to insist Danny cancel the games. He'll make it sound like it's to give the killer less of a chance to get at those kids."

Robin stared at her clenched fists. Coach Danny? But he prayed before and after every game. At one time, he'd trained for the ministry.

And Christians were tempted all the time, and sometimes they fell.

She had to see Kerry, at least, and make sure he was protected.

❦

He imagined holding her. Sam got to do it all the time, and he didn't seem to treasure the gift like he ought. Someone ought to teach him a lesson, but as the guy was in jail, he wasn't especially worried about his attitude toward Robin.

She was so beautiful, so fragile. A bird with broken wings. That's what she was. God was all about healing, and He'd picked the right man to work on Robin. He'd get her fixed up in no time. Do everything

God would have done if He'd had the time.

He laughed, low in his throat, and went back to the image of him holding her. The same vision—he'd hold her, she'd hold the baby, the two kids would be there, obedient at last, and everything would be perfect.

What was Macias doing with Sam? Imprisoning him so he could feel like he was doing something productive? Trying to prove to the island that they were safe? But they weren't. Blame Sam, feel safe, stop being so watchful. Now she had to suspect another man she knew, one she trusted. One she would have trusted with the lives of the most precious of those she loved until Donovan got to her and destroyed her faith.

Well, not Kerry. She wouldn't let anyone get to him. That one, she had to protect.

She found Kerry at home with his mother.

Mrs. Wright let Robin in and led her to the living room. "He's been crying ever since Danny called with the news. He swears Sam couldn't have done anything bad to anyone."

"I agree with him." Robin sat down on the couch, pushing herself back into its softness. Someone would have to haul her out, but she'd worry about that later.

While she waited for Mrs. Wright to bring Kerry from his room, she looked around. It was a sweetly decorated room, full of flowers and lace, but not overwhelmingly so. Robin hadn't gotten much of a chance to see it before, filled as it had been with people. Now, she wondered about Kerry's space. Did his mother let him cover the walls with pictures of the team? Had Kerry hung any of the pictures that Donovan took on his walls? Of course, he'd have pictures of his beloved coach on the wall. She shivered.

Someone else was responsible for the terror the island was experiencing. It wasn't Sam, and she couldn't make herself believe it was Danny. It was...someone else. And no one was safe.

She'd have to spend a lot of time reminding herself of that.

"Robin!" Kerry stumbled into the room. His light brown hair stood up in rumpled misery, and his face twisted with agony. He threw himself onto the couch next to her. Robin stroked his hair, murmuring nonsense.

After a few minutes, he straightened and grabbed her hand. "They said Sam did all those bad things." His voice was full of conviction and fear.

"They said that, yeah." And it had broken her heart as badly as it had Kerry's.

"How could he do that?" He sat up and grabbed her blouse. Fresh tears poured down his face.

Robin wiped at his cheek with one hand and cupped his face. "He didn't. Kerry, you *know* Sam. He's a good man. He wouldn't do something like that."

"They why doesn't he tell them?"

"I'm sure he has." She looked over his shoulder at Kerry's mother.

Mrs. Wright shook her head. "He's been like this since we heard."

"I can understand. I've felt the same way." Robin closed her eyes. *Please God, help me to make this right. Kerry doesn't need this, and I don't, and for sure, Sam doesn't. But someone does.*

"You were on TV." Kerry's eyes narrowed now in

accusation. "I heard you, Robin. You said you thought he did it."

"No, I didn't. I was very careful not to say that, because it's not true. But I wanted to fool some people."

"Who? You fooled me, Robin. Why'd you want to fool me?" Why did she have to break his heart to heal him? It wasn't fair.

"Not you, Kerry." She gave his shoulder a tiny shake just to make him realize how much she meant it. "I wanted to fool the killer."

"You know who the killer is? Who's the killer, Robin?"

Robin sighed. "I don't know. That's the problem. If I did, you better believe I'd tell the police." And she couldn't tell Kerry anything. Warn him away from Danny? It would send him right to the coach, protesting, begging for reassurance. And that would put him in danger. Keeping him in the dark was just as bad, but she couldn't help that. She had to risk it. Until she had the killer in a corner and he had no other way to get out than through her. "I have to ask you some questions."

"OK." Kerry looked at his mother. "She has to ask me some questions, and she doesn't believe Sam did anything bad."

"I'm glad she doesn't." Mrs. Wright smiled, though her eyes gleamed with moisture.

"Kerry, look at me." When he did, his brown eyes full of angry tears, Robin went on. "I need you to tell me all over again about the day Donovan saved you."

"Oh, you want to know about the bad guy." He nodded. "Yeah. He was a real bad guy. He snuck up behind me, and he would've grabbed me if Donovan hadn't come and saved me. He would've killed me like all the other people." His eyes grew wide, and tension tightened his face muscles.

"Did he grab you?"

Kerry bounced like an exclamation point to his words. "No. Donovan did, to save me."

Robin shook her head. "But the bad guy didn't touch you?"

"Nope. Donovan didn't give him a chance. Wasn't that good? He saved me, Robin. He didn't let the bad guy grab me."

"OK." Robin swallowed. "So what did the bad guy look like?"

Kerry shrugged, his arms flailing with the effort. "I dunno. He ran away. He ran when Donovan yelled at him. I didn't even know he was there, Robin. If Donovan didn't come, he'd've got me."

Mrs. Wright stood and came to the couch. "I'm sorry Kerry can't help you. But Donovan saw him, you know. He gave the police a description. You can see it on the police blotter website." Her stance told Robin she wanted her to stop pestering Kerry with questions.

"I've seen it." And it looked a little too much like Sam for Robin's taste. She frowned. "When it first happened, the police said you saw him."

"No, I didn't. Donovan thought I did. He kept saying I did, even though I said no. But that's OK, Robin. He was scared, too. Just like me. I was real scared."

"I was pretty scared, too, and by the time I heard about it, I already knew you were safe." She gripped his hands in hers. And now she didn't know that he would remain safe, and that tore her apart.

"Yeah. 'Cuz Donovan saved me."

If it had been Coach Danny, Donovan would have recognized him right away. He'd have told the police, wouldn't he? Unless he thought he needed to protect him.

Her hands shook with the strain of trying to figure things out.

Robin made herself nod. "Listen, Kerry, you have to be really careful. I mean it. The police keep saying everyone is safe now since Sam is in jail. But you know that's not right, don't you?"

Kerry's jaw dropped, and his words were a near howl. "We're not safe?"

"No, we're not. We're not safe at all. Remember, Sam didn't do anything bad. That means the bad guy isn't in jail and that the police don't care." Oh, they didn't, not at all. Robin wanted to scream with the anger and frustration of it all.

"So what do we do?" Kerry, eyes wide and terrified now, looked from her to his mother. "Mom, what do we do? I don't wanna get grabbed. I don't wanna get killed!"

"You have to keep yourself safe." Robin glanced at Mrs. Wright before concentrating on Kerry. He was the one she had to convince. "You have to stay with your mom and dad all the time, Kerry. *All* the time. Don't go away with anybody. You hear me? Not even me. Just because you think you can trust someone doesn't mean they're good, OK?"

"OK." Kerry nodded. "I get it. Nowhere but with my mom or dad. What about Sam?"

"Sam's not here, Kerry. They aren't going to let him out until they know for sure he didn't do anything bad, and they won't know it unless they catch the bad guy doing something wrong. And I don't want it to be you that the bad guy hurts."

Kerry's brows drew together. He didn't get it. Not really.

Robin's stomach twisted with fear.

"Kerry. The bad guy. He wants me, I think. And I'm going to be really careful." To catch him, anyway. "But maybe he knows how much I love you. He watches me, I think, and he knows who my best friends are. He might want to hurt you to make me pay attention to him. I don't want him to."

"Me, either!"

"Good. So you'll stay with Mom *all* the time? You won't go away with *anyone* else, no matter how good you think they are?"

Kerry nodded, kept nodding so hard he slipped and almost fell from the couch.

Robin boosted him back up. "That's all I need to hear." *And please, God, it was enough.* She grinned at him. "I'm going to need some help getting out of your couch though. It's trying to swallow me."

Kerry laughed and stood up. Between him and his mother, Robin escaped the piece of furniture.

Mrs. Wright held out her hands. "Why don't you stay for lunch, Robin?"

After a deep breath, Robin nodded. A half hour more wouldn't matter much. At least now, she knew Kerry was safe.

She needed strength. Strength from both God and nutrition. She needed to think before she put herself out there again. "OK, thanks. I really appreciate it."

Mrs. Wright smiled and left for the kitchen.

Robin took a chance. "Hey, Kerry, do you have pictures up in your room? Or posters? Baseball players?"

"Yeah, sure, I got us." Kerry grinned and bounced on the couch. "Wanna see? Come on, Robin, I can show you. Hey, Mom, I'm gonna show Robin all my pictures, 'K?"

Robin followed him down the hall and into the small, bright room still decorated like an eight-year-old's hideaway. Pennants lined one wall, and another was full of photos held up with tape.

In the middle was the team photo Donovan had taken. "See, there's me. And there's Coach Danny. I'm right up next to Coach Danny, see?"

Robin couldn't help a shudder going through her, at the thought of precious Kerry standing next to a possible murderer. She tried to smile as Kerry went on.

"And there you are, Robin. I never had a picture of you before. I told Donovan I didn't, and he said he'd give me one."

"Of me?" She hadn't posed for Donovan other than with the team. He hadn't asked her to.

"See? Here it is. My own picture of Robin. 'Cuz you're one of my best friends, Robin. Just like you said." Kerry pointed to the picture frame next to his bed.

Robin edged forward, let one crutch fall against her leg and reached for the frame.

Donovan had cropped her face, all right, but not from one of the team pictures. He'd taken it the day she and Sam were playing on the beach.

She recognized the clothing she was wearing, a soft green button down shirt under a deep peacock sweater. Beyond that, her head was nestled against Sam's striped shirt.

One couldn't have known that, though, or that they'd been on the beach, because Donovan had cut the photo down so closely, it showed mostly just her face, and her hair, wind-whipped across her cheeks. He hadn't taken it from the cliffs, either, but from somewhere closer, somewhere on the same level, as if looking straight on at her. Which meant he'd come down to the beach to take pictures of her long before he'd let her and Sam know he was there.

"This is a nice picture." She put it back and gripped the crutch again, puzzled, but before she could put her thoughts together, the door swung the rest of the way open.

"Lunch is ready." Mrs. Wright stood in the doorway. "Now, Kerry, remember your manners."

"Right." Kerry hurried to the door, and though it was already open, he stood next to it and waved Robin through and scurried around her to the dining room, where he pulled out a chair.

She had to grip his arm when he lost his balance and teetered, but still, his gentlemanly behavior touched her heart and she praised him loudly and long.

After they'd said grace and started to eat, Robin glanced at Kerry's mother and reached out and gripped her arm. "Mrs. Wright, I'm very serious about you keeping Kerry with you all the time. You can't trust anyone."

"I understand." Mrs. Wright offered a plate of pickles, at which Robin shook her head. "You're not saying names."

"No, I'm not. I don't know any." She looked up at the older woman. Her hands clamped together in her lap and she couldn't swallow the bite of salad she'd just taken. "I don't know who's doing this any more than the police do. We know it's not Sam. Isn't that enough?"

"I guess it has to be."

She turned to Kerry. "Look, Kerry, remember when Sam and I told you to stay with your mom? That you can't trust anybody?"

He screwed up his eyes, thinking hard. "Yeah."

"OK, so you know you can't go off with anybody. Even if I come to get you, you say, no, I can't go."

"Why not? You're my friend." Tears pooled and spilled from his eyes. "You promised!"

She'd have to hold her heart together with duct tape, it was so broken. "I know, Kerry, and someday, that's going to be true again. But we don't want you to get hurt."

He frowned. "So you just promise you won't hurt me, and I can go with you, right?"

"No." Only when he flinched did Robin realize she'd shouted. "Look, Kerry. Think of all the people you trust. Mom and Dad, and your sister. You can go anywhere with them, OK?"

He nodded, wiping his face with the back of his good hand.

"Anybody else, you stay away from, unless Mom or Dad say it's OK. Your teachers should be OK." And since she didn't know any of them, they probably weren't the murderer.

"And Coach Danny, and Aaron, and the other guys and runners, and—"

"No."

He jerked to stare at her. "Huh? Whatcha mean, no?"

"I mean, no. You can't go with any of those people. Not by yourself. Not Aaron, not the team, not Coach Danny."

Kerry's face twisted and his eyes threatened to tear up again. "But why? Coach Danny's my coach. He can't do any bad things to me."

Mrs. Wright leaned across the table, laying her hand on Robin's. "I'll explain it all to him. But I'm afraid he's getting too confused right now to remember any of this."

That meant she'd have to upset him again just to make sure he understood.

Mrs. Wright pointed at Kerry's plate. "Finish up, Kerry, and tell me how Robin liked your room."

Kerry gulped and picked up his fork. "I showed Robin the picture Donovan gave me. The one of just Robin. She liked it." Kerry stopped crying and took another bite.

"Did she now?" Mrs. Wright's expression told how little she trusted Kerry's assessment of Robin's reaction.

"He takes lots of pictures. He likes pretty things. Especially you, Robin. You're so pretty, and he likes things that are pretty. But he's sad you have bad legs. He's sad I do, too. I mean, he's sad I have one bad leg." Kerry frowned at his left leg encased in its brace.

Robin bit her lip before she said, "He doesn't seem to like it when people have disabilities."

"He wants to fix us. He wishes he could."

Robin watched Kerry struggle with the words he repeated until his mother got up to put her arm around him.

"It's OK, Kerry. Robin understands, don't you?" She pierced Robin with a clear demand to agree.

"I do. I really do." But she wasn't sure that was true.

13

Robin got back in her cart, but instead of turning onto her street, she headed for the harbor. She parked in a tiny lot behind the co-op and pulled out her crutches. A restless spirit seemed to drive her to the water, but the cold, and her lack of a warmer sweater, kept her from getting closer than the boardwalk in front of the shops and restaurants.

Donovan found her on the fountain, awkwardly kicking her heels against the concrete. She had been watching him as he came down the hill and knew as soon as he saw her.

"Robin." He sat next to her, his back board straight, only his upper body turned toward her. He put his hand on top of hers, where she gripped the rounded edge of the fountain, and she let herself finally relax.

"Robin," he repeated. "I have to apologize." He seemed to swallow, though his throat didn't move. "I have to admit, when they first arrested Sam, I was glad. Overjoyed." He lifted his hand, fingers splayed defensively. He ran his hand through his hair, barely ruffling the impeccable strands before they fell back into place. "Look, I really like you, Robin. But with Sam always around, I thought—well, so I was glad when they threw him in jail. Hoped they'd convict him." He laughed, as though she ought to find his admission as humorous as he did.

He shook his head. "But it's like you don't—I mean, you're so sad."

She gaped at him. "Of course I'm sad. I'm devastated."

"I get that. Really." He stared at his jiggling knees. His back, still straight, formed an awkward angle to his neck. "But you're going to have to get over him."

Robin gasped, unable to hide her reaction. "Don't. Don't even start with that."

She pushed herself to the edge of the fountain's lip, ready to slide off, stalk away as haughtily as a pair of crutches allowed.

"Look, I'm sorry. I know you care about him." The tone in Donovan's voice stopped her rush to escape, mostly because she couldn't quite make out what it meant. "I know you don't believe he's the killer. And because you don't, well, like I said before, I don't, either." He stared at his hands and looked up at her. "I hate to see you so unhappy. I've been giving it a lot of thought, and I think I can help."

"How?"

"Remember, I'm the one who gave evidence that might have—well, the guy who went after Kerry looked like Sam, but it wasn't him. I would have recognized him. So if I tell that Macias fellow it's not Sam..."

"But if he looked like Sam, it can't have been Danny, like you thought, could it?"

"Mmm. I suppose not, but there's no saying that guy had anything to do with the murders. Anyway, I'll tell Macias, OK?"

His words trailed away as he watched Robin from under slanted lashes.

"That would be a start." Wind whipped a spray

from the fountain across the back of Robin's neck, and she shivered.

"I'll do that." He pulled out his cell and dialed.

After a few cryptic comments, he snapped it shut and grinned at her. "They want me to come sign a statement."

"Good." She turned away and back. "Thanks, Donovan. It means a lot to me, that you're sticking up for Sam. For me, too."

"Sure. Anytime. You gotta know I'd do just about anything for you." He nodded, still grinning, and hurried away.

Robin watched him until he turned up the street leading to the police station.

Too bad she couldn't love the man. He truly cared. She'd never forget that.

৵৽৽

Now the restless spirit wanted her fingers to call the police station. To check on how Donovan's statement affected Sam. But she had her shift that afternoon, so she shook off her unease and started for the co-op.

Grams was ambling along the waterfront and stopped when she saw Robin. "Look what I got at the market." She opened one of her carrier bags for Robin to peek inside. "Pumpkins. Aren't they the cutest things? I've never seen them so round and perfect and tiny."

"They're great, Grams." Even though Grams' use of the word "perfect" made Robin shudder, she managed to hide it. "I'll help you decorate when I get back."

"Are you working this afternoon?"

"Yeah. I traded with Grace. I wanted Friday night free."

"Why? You got a date?" Grams started to laugh, looked at Robin's face, and sobered immediately. "I'm sorry, kiddo. That was really insensitive. You're missing Sam, I know. I shouldn't tease you."

Robin blinked and looked away. "No, you shouldn't."

"I said I was sorry."

"I know." Robin twisted her lips enough that it might, she hoped, look like a smile. "It's OK. You're right. I really miss him. I wish he was here." So desperately she might give in to the tears if she didn't get hold of herself. Once again, the spirit of unrest prodded her between her shoulder blades, pushing her to fly away.

Grams tucked the bag under her arm. "How long a shift did you take?"

"Just two hours. I'll be back a little after four."

"All right. I'll plan an early dinner. I'm sure you're going to be tired."

So was Robin. She went on her way, stopping a few times to greet neighbors and friends, and by the time she got to the store, Grace was ready to go. She barely said hello and good-bye, and gave Robin a long hug before she was gone, leaving Robin in the almost empty shop.

Not quite empty. Three women wandered the aisles, exclaiming over the displays, and loading their own arms and each other's with craft items. Robin grinned and offered to let them pile everything on the counter until they were ready to check out.

As the three women continued shopping, Robin

couldn't help overhearing their conversation.

"I heard they let him work with some kids. Handicapped kids, on a sports team. And they never knew!" The woman leaned toward her friends, and her gray curls bobbed with the violence of her feelings.

Her eyes were wide and wild, and Robin wanted to snatch every piece of merchandise out of her hands and shove her out the door. Preferably all the way into the harbor, which was cold and gray and almost as stormy as the woman's eyes, though not nearly as angry as Robin felt. They had no idea they were discussing the man who held Robin's heart, the man she would trust her life to.

"I heard he had an alibi." The shortest of the three frowned. She held up a necklace of gray, glowing stones, at the bottom of which hung a dolphin. After she checked the price tag, she sighed and draped it over the necklace stand. "I always thought a good alibi got you off, but I suppose not."

Robin looked down at her hands, one squeezed around a pen and the other clutching an order form. The pen snapped, and she dropped the pieces, as well as the crumpled paper, onto the floor behind the counter. If she could tell them, just explain—but she had no real proof. Not yet. That depended on Donovan.

The women went on gossiping. "I'm just glad they've got the killer behind bars. Those poor people. The way he desecrated their bodies."

"And think of their families." Another of the women reached across the counter and set a stack of postcards on top of her pile. "I think I'm ready, dear. How about you two?"

Robin rang up their purchases and bagged the

items in the co-op's signature ocean-wave decorated sacks. As glad as she was for their business, she wasn't at all sad to see them go.

The rest of her shift followed much the same pattern. People came in, made their selections, and talked about Sam's arrest, as though they were all integral members of the little island town. Some probably were, although Robin didn't recognize them. And she was glad of it. Because they'd know her, and they might remember who the victims had been decked out to look like. She didn't want that kind of recognition.

As she dragged her weary body out the door, after turning over the shop to the next artist, she saw Donovan. She could only nod at him and lean on her crutches. She hadn't taken three steps from the shop but already she was panting.

"Hey, Robin. I didn't know you had a shift today. You look wiped out."

"I am, but that's OK. I needed a distraction."

He nodded, clearly not taking in her words. "Look, I went right to the police, talked to Macias, like I said." He slanted an ice-blue glance at her. "He thanked me, said it was good to know, he'd take it under advisement. But he couldn't let Sam go yet. Sounded like he had something else on him."

Robin sighed. So much for getting Sam out of jail.

"I'm sorry. I was really hoping. For you, you know."

She forced a twist of lips to imitate a smile. "Thanks. I appreciate it."

He nodded, matching his slouching walk to her speed. After a minute, he turned, and this time she felt the full potency of his attention.

"You usually take the Friday night shift, right?"

"Right." She forced herself to add, "Date night."

"You've got a date for Friday?" He dropped half a step behind her as she headed away from the harbor.

Of course not, she thought. *Sam is in jail.* But he hadn't asked, even though he'd hinted at wanting to, and she didn't want to think about why he hadn't. She might lose some of her tenuous hope if she did.

"Not yet." She had to change the subject. It was so hard to keep Donovan on her wavelength. "I was over at Kerry's house the other day. We were talking about your pictures."

He grinned. "The team pictures, yeah. They turned out really great, didn't they? You never picked up your copy. I could bring it over for you later. Won't take but a little while to print it out."

"Sure, any time would be fine. No hurry. But back to the pictures you gave Kerry. I was thinking more of the other one."

He'd been keeping pace beside her, slowing his steps to match hers. Now, he turned, and the fierceness of his movements made her jerk back. "What other one? Who says I took other pictures?"

"Donovan, you walk around town with a camera. Everyone knows you take pictures. Why's that such a big deal?"

His face cleared, and his shoulders lost some of their pugnacious hold. "OK, right. But I don't know what other pictures you're talking about."

She slanted a questioning look at him. "The one you gave Kerry, of me."

"Oh, that. Right. Funny, I forgot about that." He stared straight ahead, but a muscle jumped in his jaw.

Robin turned up her street.

Donovan followed, chuckling now. "Like you said, I carry a camera around town with me. Everyone knows I take pictures. I can't remember every shot."

She shrugged as best she could while gripping the crutches and maneuvered around a fire hydrant. "I guess I can understand that. I don't exactly remember every mermaid I've ever made."

"But those were good pictures. You were having a good time." He caught up with her and glanced at her. "That doesn't happen often enough, does it?"

"What?" She frowned. "Having a good time? I have fun every single day I'm alive."

"Oh, come on. You expect me to believe that? When you're running out of breath just trying to get home after work?"

Hot words filled her mind, but she refused to engage them. Her life, the quality of it, was none of his business. She angled her way to a nearby cut in the curb and edged her way to the street. After checking for traffic and seeing the road empty of any golf carts, she started across.

Donovan followed. "Look, I'm not trying to make you feel bad. But don't think I don't know how it is. You're wanting to be normal, but your legs won't let you. They call it putting up a brave front, right? Isn't that what you're doing?"

"Actually, no." Robin gripped the crutches tighter and swung herself harder along the street. So what if she was out of breath. She didn't consider herself broken or damaged. Not now, not anymore. Donovan, in all his arrogance and condescension, had taught her that, at least.

Funny how God had used him to teach her.

"No, really. I know better. Just like with that kid,

that Kerry. He talks nonsense all the time. Can't walk right and can barely pronounce one word in twenty. And he thinks he's perfect."

Robin stopped within a foot of the opposite curb to round on the man. "He. Is." The words scraped through her gritted teeth.

His eyes widened, and he backed up a step. "How can you say that? Anyone can look at him and see he's not right."

"Donovan, that's a really horrible attitude. Yes, Kerry has handicaps. I'm not denying that. So do I. But that doesn't make us damaged, and it doesn't make us worthless either."

His mouth dropped open, and he stared at her for several, eon-length seconds before he recovered, stammering. "Look, no, I never said you were worthless. No. You're one of the best—you, and Kerry, too. He's a great guy. But you can't go around pretending you're happy with your handicaps. That's ridiculous."

"You don't get it, do you?"

"Sure, I get it. I see you all the time. I see him. I see the other kids. I see how hard it is. I wish I could do something to make you better. That's all, Robin." Passion twisted his features. "I just want you to be perfect, to have perfect lives. What's wrong with that?" He pounded the side of a fist against his temple. "You're the one who doesn't get it, Robin. You don't understand. I'm trying so hard to show you, but you just won't." For the first time, she saw emotion in his ice-colored eyes.

But there was so much wrong with his words.

"Listen to me. If my legs worked just fine, I wouldn't be on the team. I wouldn't know all the kids, all my teammates, and the runners, and the people who come to support us. I wouldn't know Kerry. And that would handicap me far more than not being able to run."

But his expression didn't change from fierce determination to any kind of understanding.

She looked up and saw her front door. "Look, I'm home, and I'm tired. I'll see you sometime, OK?"

Donovan glanced over at the house. "You use crutches and live in a two-story building?"

"That's right. Bye." Robin banged up the steps and unlocked her front door.

He wanted to help.

Couldn't she just let go of her anger enough to let him?

❧

Becca and Jake both stared when Mr. Bird came in with the new clothes. Becca didn't feel like moving, and anyway, it was her turn to hide the hole. Jake kept telling her they had to make it deeper, not wider. She didn't get it until he showed her with a pile of dirty sheets. So now she leaned against the wall, her thumb in her mouth.

Mr. Bird dropped the paper bag and held up a sweater. It was bright, blue or green, and it looked soft.

Becca wanted to lay down on it, and wrap it around her. The sheets weren't very warm and she almost always had goose bumps on her arms and legs.

"Remember the job you're going to do for me? This is what you're going to wear. Pretty, isn't it? It's almost the same color as my little robin's eyes."

Becca didn't want to wear it anymore.

He squatted in front of her. "What's the matter, little robin? You're getting pale. Are you sick?"

She stared at his face and sucked her thumb.

He shook his head and gathered the clothes together. "I'll keep these safe. Don't want them getting all dirty in here. But you'll get to wear them when we finish off the story. That won't be long. I promise."

After Mr. Bird went away again, Jake crawled onto the bed next to Becca. "Don't you let him beat you down. Don't you let him."

Without taking her thumb out of her mouth, Becca said, "He din' hi' me."

"I'm not talking about him hitting you." Jake put his arm around her. Nobody had touched her in so long, and Becca leaned into his skinny chest. "I mean, don't let him make you give up. Don't stop trying."

"But I'm too scared to try." She dug her head into his chest. "I'm so scared."

❧❦

With Sam as her protector gone, it seemed Robin ran into Donovan everywhere: at the co-op, at the grocery store, leaving church on Sunday morning.

"I've been thinking," he said after she'd left after the service. He stuck his hands in the pockets of his baggy slacks. "We can't prove Sam isn't the killer because he hasn't got all the alibis he needs."

Robin stared at her crutch tips and nodded.

"The only way to clear him is to prove it's someone else."

He said the words as though he'd never considered the possibility before. But they'd gone over it countless times, and Robin sighed. Repeating what they needed to do didn't get it done.

"I thought you agreed?"

Robin stopped, straightening to glare at him. "I thought we were going to do something."

"Well, yeah. When we figure out what." He turned, looking her. "The thing is, whoever it is has a thing for you. I don't know if you'd worked that out." His gaze slanted towards her. "I mean, he made the dead bodies look like you. I already told you that."

"We discussed it, yes. I remember." She shifted a crutch. "And Alan Bricker told me, and Macias keeps reminding me. Didn't they question you just because you know me?"

"Well, yeah."

She edged over dry grass at the edge of the walkway to pass him, and he immediately started to walk alongside her again.

"So they looked at everyone you know?"

She nodded.

"That's how they got onto Sam?"

"They didn't tell me."

The church lot, usually full of golf carts after a service, had emptied, leaving only a few. Reluctantly, Robin asked, "Do you need a ride?"

"It's too beautiful a day to waste in a vehicle. Anyway, you need the exercise."

Clenching her teeth, Robin ground out, "I get plenty of exercise."

"Yeah, but if you didn't use crutches, you could take walks and get fit like anybody else. And better than that, we could hold hands while we walked."

She might be able to hold hands with Sam, too. But then, she'd have no reason to lean into his embrace every time she went up to bat. Robin stowed her crutches in the hold and lifted herself into the cart.

Why did she need this guy anyway? Sure, he promised to help her clear Sam, but it wasn't his job any more than it was hers. Macias had made that clear.

"Robin?"

"Later, OK?"

"Wait." He gripped the roof of the cart and swung himself inside.

Robin let out a breath of frustration but didn't ask him to get out. He wasn't bad, just colossally insensitive.

"Just FYI." She spun the cart to head for the road leading to the town center and her grandmother's house. "Even if I could, I wouldn't hold your hand."

"Oh, understood." He chuckled. "You're Sam's girl."

She went up over the curb. With a struggle, she coaxed the cart back onto the road.

Donovan waited until they were underway again, and said, "You made it sound like you don't think I'm doing anything to help. But I've been making some lists. I want to show them to you."

She let the cart stall and stared at him.

"Really. Here. I got them with me." He reached into a back pocket and pulled out a crumpled mass of lined paper, which he unfolded. "Remember I said to watch Danny? Here's all the reasons why. Here. Look at this one." He pointed to some scrawled words, and despite her inner shrinking away from that idea, Robin leaned forward to read them.

6. Acts like Robin is his property. Uber protective. Forgets she's an adult who can make her own decisions.

Robin frowned. "There's nothing wrong with this, Donovan. He's protective of all the team members."

"Yeah, well, the rest of them are kids."

"No, they're not. Have you even looked at them?"

"What do you think? I take pictures of them all the time. I told you, Robin. I see things other people don't." He gave her a look full of significance she couldn't read. "I see things."

She flipped the start button on the cart and pulled it back onto the road. "First you accused Sam without having much of a reason, and now you're stuck on Danny."

She pulled into the small parking area in front of her grandmother's house. "You can make it to wherever you're going, right?" Since he'd just touted the benefits of walking, she didn't feel the need to coddle him.

"Sure." He put one leg out of the cart and leaned back in, moving fast.

Only seconds before his mouth reached hers, Robin realized his intentions and turned her head.

"Hey! You let Sam kiss you!"

Rather than demand how he knew, she pointed to the street. "That's enough. You should go now."

❧❦

At four fifty that afternoon, Sam looked up to see a warden, followed by Detective Macias, stop outside his cell door. He was alone in the jail. In the last three days two kids, both high on meth, had been admitted and released, and several drunks had spent time in the tank. Sam had been the only constant, and though they hadn't formally charged him with kidnapping and murder, he knew it was just a waiting game. One he didn't want to play.

"Detective." He stood and shoved his hands in his pockets.

"Sam." The man motioned to the warden, who opened the cell and stepped back.

Sam raised his eyebrows. They were setting him free? Odd. He didn't move.

"Come on out." Macias waved a large hand and moved out of Sam's way.

"What's going on?"

"We can only hold you for seventy-two hours without charging you, but we don't have enough evidence." Macias glared at him as though Sam had arranged to hide evidence solely to thwart him.

"But I'm still a suspect."

"Number one." Macias seemed to be biting the inside of his mouth.

"So you're just going to let me go?" Sam edged out of the door, past the warden, who slammed it after him. The relief of knowing he was on the outside filled his chest with happiness and something more, something that seemed to have sprouted wings, but the look on the detective's face warned him to keep his celebration hidden, at least for a while.

Macias glowered at him, his head bent so his brows looked heavy and menacing. "You'll be under surveillance. If I were you, I'd line up my alibis really carefully. Make sure you're with someone at all times."

Sam snorted. "I'm single. You suggesting I go shack up with someone every night just to stay out of jail?"

"I'm suggesting you make sure no one can pin it on you. Either that, or make sure no one else gets kidnapped or killed."

Sam watched the warden disappear into the break

room and followed Macias to the front of the police station. "What are you saying?"

Macias said nothing while Sam's things were returned to him. A few minutes later, Sam was once again dressed in his own clothing and out in the open air. The sunshine he'd been missing had disappeared, and heavy clouds rolled across the sky. He didn't care. A storm, while he was free and outside to experience it, was a thousand times more precious than sunshine he couldn't feel.

As soon as the heavy doors closed behind them, Macias said, "Sam, Bricker admitted he'd told you."

"He did? When?"

Macias turned and stared hard into Sam's eyes. He'd stuffed his hands into his jacket pockets and gestured with his hands surrounded by material. "When I asked him. Three days ago."

Fury started a small fire in Sam's chest. "You said he denied it."

"Yeah, I did. But there's still the question of that baby. You found her where we'd already searched. So I put you in jail."

"I told you I had a feeling."

"I think you had prior knowledge. Unfortunately, that's all I have on you at the moment, but I swear, Albrecht, I'll be watching you."

14

Becca squatted by the door with her thumb in her mouth and watched Jake. He crouched next to her mattress, bent tight like a ball, and scraped the hole with the handle of her toothbrush. He'd already broken his in half. But the hole was huge now, big enough that she could have crawled through it, if there was anywhere to go. But there wasn't. Instead, bits of wood stopped her. When Becca first ran into all that wood, she'd thrown her toothbrush at Jake and cried.

Jake had tried to break the strips. He'd tried kicking them. He'd said a couple words that made Becca look over her shoulder, waiting for someone to yell at him. No one did, of course. Mr. Bird hadn't been there since the night before, and her stomach rumbled.

Something snapped, and with another string of words, Jake flopped onto his back on the mattress, two more bits of toothbrush handle in his hands.

Becca popped her thumb out for a minute. "Are you gonna give up?"

"No, I'm not gonna give up." He stood up, glared at the wall for a few minutes, pushed the mattress back in place, shoved her pillow over the dust and pushed the sheets over it. Now it just looked like a messy bed. And it looked like he was giving up after all.

"What are you gonna do?"

"Stop whining." He sat down on his mattress and jerked his hand at her. "You don't have to listen for a while, OK? I'm gonna think."

She got up and stood in the middle of the room, watching him. He put his knees up, and leaned his arms on them with his head tipped back against the wall.

She stepped closer. "Can we pray?"

"What good's that gonna do?"

"God always answers. He loves us." That's what her mommy and daddy always told her. Just because praying made her feel bad didn't mean Jesus wasn't listening. He probably felt bad for her, too.

"Yeah, yeah. But we're still stuck in this dungeon, and nobody's helping us get out."

"We should pray anyway."

Jake shrugged and got up. "Go ahead. I'm gonna look in the bathroom again. Hey, get me the end of your toothbrush. Not the brush part, the other part. Maybe I can use that. Maybe I can dig through the wood with it. That wood's all splintery."

Becca hunkered down and felt along the wall until she grabbed the bit of plastic. The unbroken end had worn down, and the broken end was twisted. But it had a few sharp points. They might be able to do something with it.

She took it to the bathroom. "Here. I gotta go."

"OK." Jake left the bathroom and let her do what she needed to. After she washed her hands, she opened the door.

Mr. Bird had come in.

Becca plopped down on her mattress and stuck her thumb back in her mouth. What if he looked behind her pillow? What if he already knew what they were doing? What if he decided to check their toothbrushes to see if they'd been brushing their teeth?

And what if he'd caught Jake with the end of her toothbrush? She looked at Jake.

He stared up at Mr. Bird. His hands were behind his back, and he looked like he expected Mr. Bird to hit him. But Mr. Bird didn't seem interested in Jake at all.

He held out a couple sandwiches and boxes of milk with straws already in them. "You want some lunch?"

She nodded. She didn't mention not having had any breakfast, and neither did Jake.

"Listen, kids. Things are changing. I talked to both your parents—"

Jake made a face like he didn't believe anything Mr. Bird said.

"Well, your mom, anyway, and they might be coming to get you sooner than I thought. We're gonna get you two fixed up for them."

"Fixed up?" Jake put his sandwich down on the floor and stared up at Mr. Bird.

"Yeah. Haircuts, and some new clothes. Stuff like that." Mr. Bird reached down and stroked Becca's messy head. "I'm going to put something in your hair to make it not so tangled. It'll turn it black but that's OK. That'll go away."

"No." Jake stood up.

"What?" Mr. Bird looked mean when he turned to Jake.

"No, you're not gonna dye her hair."

"No, you're right, I'm not. It's for the tangles."

"You're lying." Jake glared up at Mr. Bird like he wanted to punch him. His hands made tight fists that he pressed to his sides. "You're planning to dye her hair just like you did to Lehanie, but I'm not gonna let you."

"Like you could do anything." Mr. Bird shook his head. "Stupid kid."

Becca gasped, and Mr. Bird's hand pressed down on the top of her head.

"Your hair's as bad as Becca's," Mr. Bird went on. "It's all tangled. I'm gonna have to do something about that, too."

"Give me a brush and I'll take care of both of us."

Mr. Bird laughed. It didn't sound nice, like when Becca's daddy laughed. It sounded like the kid on the bus who made fun of Becca's brother when he cried.

Mr. Bird didn't say anything else. He left them in the room again, and Becca heard the sound of the lock. Jake didn't even try the door after he left. Mr. Bird never forgot, never made a mistake about that lock.

Jake sat back down and put his head on his knees. After a minute, he looked up. "You better eat," he said. "And drink all your milk."

"OK." She took a bite. "Aren't you gonna eat?"

"Yeah." Jake ate his sandwich is three bites and gulped down his milk. He threw the carton in the corner, on top of all the other stinky trash and went back to his mattress. He didn't sit down, though. Instead, he knelt on the concrete floor and started pulling at the edge of his mattress.

"Do you want me help you move it?" Becca asked. "What are you doing? Are you gonna try to dig another hole over there?"

"No. Be quiet. I'm trying to rip it open." Jake leaned down and bit the striped cover. Over and over, he'd bite, jerk his head, ripping the fabric. After a few minutes, he made a long hole in the cover. After that, he ripped at it with his hands.

"Why are you doing that?" Becca finished her

sandwich and went to stand next to him.

"'Cuz I was thinking. There's stuff inside mattresses. Springs and wires and stuff. If I can get some of them out, we can dig with them."

"And you can hide the hole just like we did with the hole in the wall."

"Right."

She sat down to watch. He pulled out lots of fluffy stuff that wouldn't help anybody, and finally made a noise that let her know he'd found what he wanted.

But no matter how hard he pulled, or how he tried to twist the pieces inside his mattress, he couldn't get anything to come out. Everything was all wound together, tight.

When Jake threw himself down on the mattress and put his arm over his eyes, Becca climbed up next to him. She wriggled around until she could stroke his hair. He didn't push her hand away.

"I'm gonna pray now."

"OK." Jake's voice sounded funny.

"God, I'm scared. I think Jake is scared, too, even though he won't say it. Can You help us, please?"

Jake didn't say anything else, and Becca went on stroking his head for a long time.

⇦⇨

Since his phone had gone dead in the three days he'd been incarcerated, Sam first went home to plug it in. Then he headed to Robin's. He found her in the garden in back of the house. She leaned over the wall that separated her grandmother's property from the street and looked out at the harbor. From that position, she could probably only see the tops of the sailboat masts, and maybe a hint of blue-gray and choppy white, but as much as she loved the ocean, it might be enough.

Something about the way she was standing, with her crutches dropped to her sides and her elbows atop the wall, her shoulders hunched as she stared out to sea, caught at Sam's heart. She was beautiful. He'd always known that. Now, his heart knew something more.

And he didn't want to acknowledge it. Because if he did, if he let himself realize how much she meant to him, he wouldn't be able to protect her. Hadn't he failed the last time someone's life depended on him? He wasn't about to set Robin up for him to let her down.

He shook his head. He couldn't think that way. Yes, his partner had died because Sam hadn't been quick enough, but Sam hadn't been the one to point the gun. And he wasn't the one targeting Robin. Just the one who wanted to keep her safe.

Still, a small part of him believed that if he gave in to his heart, he'd put her in danger.

Robin turned, shrieked his name, and grabbed for her crutches. While she scrabbled for them, he was across the tiny patio, and his arms were around her.

So much for not giving in to his heart.

"Oh, Sam, you're—you're *here*. They let you out? I mean, they don't think you're the one who—"

He brushed his lips across her hair. She smelled like the wind. "They still do. At least, Detective Macias does. He said he'll be watching me."

"What?" She leaned back, resting her weight against his arms. It felt so right. "How can he possibly think you're guilty? He's crazy."

"Unfortunately, he's the police." He held her closer, pulling her head to his chest, careful to let her keep her balance. "Looks like I'm the one who has to prove I'm innocent, and I can't do that going home alone every night. Any chance your grandmother will let me stay here at night? I can even stay on the second floor with her, if she's suspicious—" He stopped his own words. Why wouldn't she be suspicious? And of far more than Sam having designs on her granddaughter.

He helped Robin gather her crutches, which had clattered to the floor when he grabbed her, and held the door. He fetched them both sodas and jerked his head toward her bedroom. "If we go in your room and shut the door, is your grandmother going to come after me with a shotgun?"

"I doubt it." Robin shoved the door open. "An ax, maybe."

Sam stopped walking.

"I'm kidding. Honestly, I don't think she sees me as a normal human being sometimes. I don't know if it's that business where parents can't believe their children are really old enough, or if my crutches have blinded her."

"They can do that." They might have blinded Sam. But then again, he often didn't notice them. They were a bit like a favorite pair of jeans, intrinsically a part of her, something she always wore, but not especially important.

He waited for her to hoist herself onto her bed and parked himself as far away as he could get. That meant the folding chair in front of her sewing machine. He left it facing the machine, sat on it backward, and leaned his elbows on the back. As he stretched his legs out, one foot rustled the curtain of blue and blue-green beads. Their song made him smile and reminded him of Robin's story about her dad. He hadn't been perfect either, but he had loved Robin with a perfect love. He'd saved her from feeling abandoned when she needed it.

God willing, Sam would be able to save her, too, as soon as she needed it. Because it wasn't up to Sam anyway, it was up to God.

"Tell me." With both hands, Robin pulled one leg up so it folded in front of her, then the other, and she was sitting cross-legged. She had to bolster herself with pillows so she didn't topple over, but still, she looked like a teenager settling in for a long gossip with friends.

If only he could give her that kind of news.

"Macias admitted that Bricker told him he'd leaked privileged news to me. But he still thinks I knew Cynthia was in the warehouse before I found her, and the only way I'd know was if I'd put her there."

"And no one has gone missing since they arrested you. No bodies have shown up, either. Which makes everything worse."

"And as soon as everyone knows I'm out?" Sam raised his eyebrows and took a drink of soda. "Macias is announcing it right now."

"You mean, you think the murderer was waiting for you to get out so he could frame you? Make it look like you all over again?" Robin frowned. "If he does, what are you going to do?"

"That's why I want to stay here."

"Oh. I see." She looked down, her hands worrying the fringe of a blue blanket, color staining her cheeks.

"That means someone else will probably get hurt."

"It could happen." Sam nodded. "The police can't be everywhere. And there are still two kids missing."

Her head came up. "Sam, it's not right. We can't let them risk those kids!"

"No, we can't."

"How are we going to stop him?"

Sam grinned. "You think Grams is going to be OK with me staying here?"

Robin's mouth opened, and nothing came out. She closed it and blurted, "No, I really don't think she's going to be too happy about an ex-con living here with her and her granddaughter."

"I won't be living here, in your room. And technically, I'm not an ex-con."

"Yeah, well." She reached for her cell. "Let me call her and ask."

Sam shot to his feet. "You mean she's not here?"

"She's upstairs. This is how I get in touch with her when she's not on the ground floor." She punched a number and said, "Grams, Sam is here, and we need to talk to you."

After she clicked off, Sam said, "Just tell her I need to protect myself."

"Sam." Robin scooted to the edge of the bed. "We need to protect everyone. Once this guy knows you're free, everyone is in danger again."

15

He stood, tumbling the chair, but righted it as he tried to frame the words. "I know, I know, babe. I'm sorry."

She shook her head, the tears making tracks on her cheeks. "These last couple of days, people have gotten, I don't know, almost cocky. They think they're out of danger."

"They weren't."

"Wait. I think they were." She held up her hand as if reading the protest forming in his mind. "Not because I think you're the murderer. You know better than that. But maybe he was holding off doing anything, to make it look like it was you after all. And now you're cleared—"

"Not cleared, just not charged."

She nodded. "Now, he might try to frame you."

"Which is why I'm here."

"I know." She sighed, and looked up. "Oh, you'll never guess who's been helping me the last couple of days. Donovan. He felt so guilty because he thought his description of the guy who tried to grab Kerry put them on to you. Remember how everyone said the sketch looked like you? Well, he told Macias he knows you, and it wasn't you."

He sat down again, his heart thudding in dread. So much for that hug, for the kiss. So much for his heart finally letting him in on its little secret love for her. He'd already lost her to a creep. But he said nothing.

"You have no idea how thankful I am. He really has been a big help."

Gratitude was so far from what he was feeling that he couldn't find words.

"And he's been coming up with ideas. I don't think much of them, but he's trying to help you."

He couldn't keep the sarcasm from his voice. "Oh, he has another suspect? Who's the lucky guy?"

"Sam!"

He held up his hands. "Sorry. Just tell me. Who does he suspect?"

Red flooded her face. "Danny. Coach Danny. I don't think he's right, but he keeps coming up with reasons why it has to be him. No real facts, just—just ideas." Again, she blushed. What had Donovan told her?

He turned away, clenching his fists.

"Sam?" Her voice sounded small and lost.

He shrugged. He wasn't mad, and he didn't know how to explain what he felt. He still needed to protect her. And his heart was still hers.

❧◈

Robin watched the emotions close down on Sam's face and wanted to throw herself in his arms, demand he open up to her, the way he always had. But she'd just hurt him. Wounded pride, or something more? How she longed for that more, but she had no right to ask for it. "Sam, just because I trust someone else doesn't mean I've abandoned you. You're still my—my best friend, you always will be." She shook her head, pushing away the personal and focusing on the urgent. "Listen, Sam, maybe—just maybe—he can help. Can you consider that for just a minute?"

Betrayal and hurt filled his face. When he stood again, she reached for him. "Don't. Please, don't look at me that way. You don't know what it was like when Grams told me you were in jail."

Sam crossed his arms, the cold in his face as he stared down at her freezing her soul. "So you went running to Mr.-let-me-tell-you-what-I'd-do-to-pedophiles?"

She jerked, reaching for crutches that weren't close enough, wanting to get away from his accusations. "That is not fair. What's making you act like this?"

He looked away. "I just spent three days in jail for something I didn't do."

"And I spent those same three days trying to prove to Macias and everyone else that you're innocent. So why take your snit out on me?"

He kept his shoulders rigid for only a moment until his tension collapsed. "I'm sorry, babe. You're right; I shouldn't take it out on you." He finally met her gaze. "Forgive me?"

She held out her hand. "Always."

He pulled her from the bed, wrapping his arms around her and holding her as he'd done in the ocean, as though her lack of usable legs was no hardship for him.

And yet the unease of wanting to check over her shoulder, to make sure no one was watching her this time, stole much of Sam's comfort.

He rubbed his cheek against her hair. "You're my greatest champion, babe."

"I am." She leaned back, trying to put some levity

into her expression. "And I think I've been able to nudge Detective Macias into another direction."

"Oh, really? Which way?"

Robin pinched her lips together. "Well, right now he's looking at the same person Donovan suspects. Coach Danny."

Sam let his arms lower. "Are you serious?"

Miserable, she nodded. "He kept asking me about him, about the games, about the things he says." She looked up. "About how he treats the kids, and how he makes me feel." She blinked, but it didn't stop the tears from pooling in her eyes. "That was the worst part, Sam, when he asked me how I knew it wasn't Danny. And I couldn't tell him. And I could only think of all the reasons it might be."

"Did you tell him?"

"I tried not to, but I don't think I did a very good job. He's pretty good at making up his mind when you're trying to distract him."

"I noticed." He paced from the doorway to window and back, his head bowed. "And Donovan gave him some other info that made him think he was onto something."

It wasn't a question.

"He went to Macias and told him you weren't the guy who went after Kerry."

"Kind of him, wasn't it, since he was the one who told them I was."

"He's sorry about that, OK? Come on, Sam. It isn't like you to hate a person for no reason."

She stared at his unreadable face until he nodded.

"You're right, it's not like me, and I should probably give him some credit." He sat again, hooking his arms over the back of the chair. "So what's the evidence against Danny? I can't believe there is any. Robin, we've known him forever. He's devoted to the kids."

"Maybe he's too devoted."

"So you're back."

Sam turned as Grams entered Robin's room. She stood at the end of the bed, looking first at Sam with a penetrating stare before she turned to Robin. With a bit of a shrug, she said, "The police let you out, and Robin let you in, so I suppose that means you're cleared?"

"No. It means they didn't have the evidence to charge me. But I'm innocent."

"Well, we knew that, didn't we?"

Sam reached out and gripped Grams' hand while Robin let out a breath full of relief. Grams was so incredibly unpredictable, and not always supportive. But she liked Sam just fine.

"I'm going to need to stay here for a bit, if you'll allow that. I need a constant alibi." Sam glanced at Robin. Something in his eyes quickened her heart, but then it was gone, and the bleak sorrow replaced it. "On the couch, of course. Or upstairs, if you'd rather."

Grams regarded him for a long, tense minute before she nodded. "OK, if I'm going to trust you a little, I've got to trust you the whole way. As long as you need."

Sam bowed his head in thanks. "Only until the killer messes up and we catch him."

"We? You're on the police force now?"

"I've always been on their side. They just aren't on mine." Sam shook his head. "Sorry, no. I'm on my own."

Grams nodded. "No, you're not. You've got Robin, and you've got me. And best of all, you've got God.

Never forget that."

This time Sam got all the way off the chair and came to grip Grams' hand. He reached back for Robin's. His fingers were warm. Something about his touch carried promises, and hints of joy, and she would do anything for this man. She was so grateful neither one of them had to do it alone any longer.

As long as that was what Sam meant. She needed him to tell her, but now wasn't the time.

"Look, they have to blame somebody, or people are going to get on their case. And if Macias points at me, and I take the heat for a while, what does that matter? We're going to catch him, Robin." He stared down at her, hope finally filling his eyes, before he turned away.

She might have melted under the intensity. Whether he grieved for the position he'd been forced into, or for something else, she had to wait for him. Otherwise, she might fly away on daydreams. But for the moment she had Sam, and he made it all worthwhile. Loving her or not, he made it all right.

Grams headed out the door. "I suppose you two need to do some planning." She winked at Sam, but Robin caught it. She was probably meant to.

"I did a lot of planning when I couldn't do anything else," Sam said. "Tonight, we're going out to dinner. I need to be as visible as possible." He glanced at Robin.

She nodded and struggled off the bed. "But this time, we're taking my cart. I'm glad I plugged it in after church."

Twenty minutes later they were waiting in line at one of the busiest cafes on the harbor. The scent of fried fish wafted out the door, along with customers, every time it opened. Some stared at Sam. One lady grabbed her child's arm and hustled him across the walkway, nearly to the now-damp sand.

Sam wrapped his arm around her shoulders. "Hush," he whispered. "It's not worth it."

She jerked away. "It's worth it to me." And if she could chase after those people, she would, and tell them a few home truths. She hadn't hated her crutches this badly in years.

"It's not the point. Come on. We want people to know I'm out, right? Well, plenty of people are going to hear it from them." He nodded toward the shore where the family still hurried on their way. "I just hope we don't get thrown out before we get some dinner."

In that, they were lucky. They both knew the *maître de*, and while he gave Sam a searching look, he also portioned out one of his rare smiles and led them to a table near the front windows. Robin saw the bill he pocketed after he told them who their waitress would be.

"You bribed him!"

Sam winked, a half grin pulling up one side of his mouth. "All for a good cause." He straightened and turned, and Robin followed the path of his gaze.

Donovan had just walked into the restaurant.

Robin sighed. She was getting incredibly tired of Donovan. He liked her, yeah, but she couldn't return the favor.

Sam stood and waved. "Donovan, over here!"

Ice blue eyes swept past Sam to meet Robin's. She blinked, tried to clear the emotion from her face, but couldn't quite manage a smile. She hoped she at least looked welcoming, but she couldn't help a thread of resentment, that first Donovan had blamed Sam, and then Danny. That he couldn't accept her the way she was.

She shivered as Sam pulled his chair closer to Robin's, to give Donovan room.

"We're celebrating my release," Sam told him.

Donovan pursed his lips as he shifted his chair closer to Robin's side of the table before he sat down. When he did, she felt as constricted as if they'd trussed her and propped her in a barrel.

Donovan's mouth remained pinched. "They cleared you, didn't they? I told them it wasn't you."

As if they would act on his word alone. Robin pressed closer to Sam, and forced herself to relax. This was a meal out with a friend, seeing people. Simple as that.

Sam leaned around her to answer Donovan. "Not exactly. But they don't have enough evidence to charge me, so they had to let me go." Sam's knee pressed against Robin's, but she wouldn't have said anything anyway.

"Right." Donovan kept looking at Robin with his particular, piercing stare, far too intense for comfort, or for polite company. She felt dissected and looked away.

"I'm innocent." Sam paused until Donovan looked at him and went on. "They tagged the wrong guy, but they don't know it, so now they're watching me." He opened his menu with an angry flick and glared over it, at no one in particular. "It's galling."

"I bet it is." Donovan opened his menu as well and asked Robin about the selections.

She murmured something, she wasn't sure what, and because their table had no room for her to open a menu, leaned toward Sam to read his.

Sam scooted closer to her. Pretty soon she wouldn't have elbow room to eat her scallops. She glanced at Sam, and he mouthed something at her.

It's OK, or, *are you OK?*

She wasn't sure what he wanted her to know. Either way, the answer was, no. She gave a tiny shake of her head and looked up when she heard the sound of more familiar voices.

Mrs. Wright, followed by her husband, their daughter, and Kerry, had come into the restaurant. Behind them were Coach Danny and his wife.

The group stopped and stared at the three of them. Robin felt a bit like a cartoon character facing a racing steam engine. Part of her wanted to bundle Kerry out of danger. Part of her wanted to grab Danny by his shirt and explain what they were doing, so as to erase the condemnation in his eyes when he looked at Sam. Part of her wanted to relieve the blame she saw in Donovan's eyes. Part of her wanted to cry, and that part almost won the battle. She blinked, tried to move away from the table, and couldn't. They'd wedged her in.

After several years' worth of silence, which lasted a good half a minute, Danny said, "Robin, glad I saw you. I wanted you to know we're cancelling the games until further notice."

"It's not fair!" Kerry burst out.

"Kerry." His father's voice seemed to spur him on.

"It's 'cuz of you, Sam. 'Cuz they say you did bad things, but Robin said you didn't. I'm all confused, Sam. Did you do them bad things?"

"I didn't." Sam pressed his lips together but made no other move, not even to reach out to the wailing young man. "I didn't do anything to those people, and

I didn't kidnap anybody. I would never hurt anybody, especially not like that. You trust me, don't you, Kerry?"

"I did."

Robin's heart broke. "You should still trust him." She scrubbed the back of one hand under her eyes. It came away wet.

The tears stopped when Sam said, "No, he shouldn't."

Shocked, Robin stared at him, but he didn't even flicker a glance at her.

"Kerry, you shouldn't trust anybody but your mom and dad, and your sister. Got that? Not me, not Robin, no one. You stay where you're safe."

"But why? I don't get it, Sam. I don't get it." Kerry stepped forward, his twisted hands clenched, but his mother grabbed his arm, and she stared at Robin for a moment. Robin couldn't tell if her expression was meant to convey a need for reassurance or disbelief.

She turned to her husband, her voice light and strained. "Do you think we ought to call the others and tell them to meet us someplace else?"

He pointed to a large table, surrounded by at least ten chairs. "They've already set up for us. Give it a rest. He can't do anything with all these people around."

What had happened to innocent until proven guilty? What had happened to all the things Mrs. Wright had agreed to just that afternoon? But Robin had heard of this kind of betrayal before. She'd just never had to live it.

Donovan stood up. "Look, Coach, I'll be at every game if you want me to. I can run a sort of security." He gestured at Robin. "She's already asked me to replace him as her runner. It's not like he'll have any reason to be there." As if not giving Sam the dignity of his name reduced him in stature. As if no one would notice how he'd gone from being their friend to their enemy within a second.

Robin's mouth flew open to correct him, but Sam's hand on her leg stopped her. She glared at him.

He shook his head. "Let it go. It's what I want." His voice barely reached her with the sound of all the other diners, even though his mouth was only inches from her ear.

She understood, but she hated it. Why was it that, when she imagined offering herself up as bait, it didn't hurt as much as watching Sam doing the same thing? Because she didn't believe it was true, real, until she saw it? Or because she really did care more for him than she did for herself? *No greater love*, she thought and bowed her head. Neither she nor Sam were the first to sacrifice anything, but it still terrified her.

"Regardless." Danny looked everywhere but at Sam now. "For the protection of all the team, we're giving it a break. No more games until the killer is caught. Until they have the evidence they need."

"That may take a while." Donovan smirked at Sam. "Seems they can't find a single thing on him right now."

"So I've heard." Danny nodded toward their table and followed the Wrights as they sat down a few yards away.

Kerry hung back, looking agonized, until his mother sharply called his name.

"I can't believe it!" Robin glared at Donovan as he sat back down. "What is with you, turning on Sam like that? After all your talk about how you don't believe it's him, how you believe—" She stopped and forced her voice to a lower level. "And I did *not* ask you to replace Sam. I said if he couldn't make it, you could step in."

Donovan shrugged. "Same thing. You know, I think I'm going to get some of this spaghetti to go. I get hungry and hate to have to come out to eat alone all the time."

Sam watched him as he spoke to the waitress, flirting with her and charming her into adding lots of breadsticks and butter to his order.

And Robin watched Sam. The cunning in his eyes scared her. He had a plan, she could tell, and she hoped he'd share it with her before he put it into action. She needed to know, so she could back him up, at least in prayer.

Donovan smirked as he returned. "Robin, you've got to know I was just acting a part. Right?" He slapped Sam on the back before he slid back into his chair. Robin had shoved it away with one crutch; he jerked it even closer to her before he sat down. "Tricking the old coach into a false sense of security, right? It's what they do all the time. You know how they play good cop-bad cop? That was me." He grinned.

Robin closed her eyes.

When she felt Donovan's arm along the back of her chair, she wanted to duck away from the contact. Her heart burned with anger, and that wouldn't help anyone.

A pleading gaze at Sam brought no relief. He raised his eyebrows, but didn't challenge Donovan. Not that Robin was sure what she wanted. A fight? Punches thrown, bloody noses? How would that help keep Sam out of jail?

She had to force food down a too-tight throat, and pray she got to go home soon.

❧❧

Outside the restaurant, Sam debated on how to shake the other man so he could get his girl home by herself. Not that she wanted to be near the guy, but Donovan stuck to her like a starfish to a rock. And terror had made poor Robin about as immobile as said rock. Sam had never seen her give in to fear that way— not when he'd taken her parasailing, not when he'd nearly dropped her in the surf a few days before, not when Danny pitched the ball and it headed straight for her face. Eating dinner with a suspected murderer had brought their shared experiences to a whole new level, and he didn't like it.

But Donovan hurried away before they reached Robin's street, claiming he had to get his package of food to the refrigerator before it started to go bad.

Not before he bussed Robin's cheek.

She froze and rubbed the spot, but as far as Sam was concerned, she was nowhere as nauseous as she ought to be. The guy had kissed her!

Fuming, he bundled her into her cart and climbed behind the steering wheel.

"Sam?"

He jerked the engine into life and didn't answer.

She bounced next to him as he raced home, going over the twenty mile an hour limit by at least two miles, until he parked and helped her out. She refused to move toward the door.

"What was that all about?"

"Let's get inside." He glanced over his shoulder,

not so much because he was nervous, but to convince Robin she should be.

It worked. She shuddered, swung her crutches, and headed for the door. That one of those crutches barely missed his shins, he noticed, and for the first time in days a smile tugged at his mouth. He repressed it. He'd rather see Robin in a temper than immobile with fear.

She stopped again. "Look, you know how he is. He doesn't have much connection with reality when it comes to me. But it's beginning to look like you don't, either." She didn't yell, but her whisper held the intensity of a bullhorn pressed to the side of his head.

"He's a jerk. And probably a murderer." And the fact that he was encroaching on Sam's girl was his worst offense, as far as Sam could see.

"What? Where did that come from? He was trying to prove you weren't guilty, that Coach Danny is. How'd you get to blaming him?"

He stroked her cheek, and leaned around her to unlock her front door. "Put the clues together. First, he blamed me. Babe, you're the one who told me Kerry never saw the guy who tried to grab him."

"So? Donovan did..." Her voice trailed off.

"And what if there was no kidnapper? What if Donovan made it up to make himself look like the hero? And to frame me at the same time?"

She shook her head, backing away from him. "No. He went to Macias and swore the guy wasn't you."

"Sure, he did. Because you were upset, right? And he knew it. He thinks of himself as your protector. He's crazy, Robin. Can't you see that?"

She shook her head harder, staring at the floor, so her black hair fell over her face and shimmered around her shoulders.

"That's just one thing, babe. He saw us on the beach, remember? And the next day, I saw the scene he set up with his favorite medium. Exactly the same. Remember when I picked you up and held you so the waves just washed over you?"

She nodded without looking up.

"But tonight, there was just something—off—in the way he looked at you. And he bought food."

Her head jerked up. "So? I suppose even murderers have to eat."

"And so do the kids they kidnap."

One crutch clattered to the floor as her hand slapped over her mouth. Sam bent to retrieve it, handed it to her, and guided her to a chair. "Babe. I'm sorry. I know you like him."

"No, I—not really, not anymore. I just don't want to think he's a—I don't want to think he watches me like that."

Sam pursed his lips. "So you weren't leading him on? Weren't encouraging him?"

Within seconds he sensed that the question, bad enough on its own, was about to explode in his face.

Anger replaced every last trace of fear, became a slow burning fuse, and he had no idea how close it might come to its target.

"No, I wasn't." Her eyes narrowed. "But what's it to you if I do?"

He reached for her, and she lifted her arms to push him away. One crutch whacked his thigh before he disentangled it from her hand. Somehow, he managed to get his arms around her, and her head rested against his shoulder.

He'd got her where he wanted her, needed her,

but he never believed he'd get her there through an argument and an insensitive witticism.

It felt a bit like when he played her runner, and a bit not. More like playing her lover, and he liked that. He leaned down to kiss her but had only managed one gentle caress on her forehead when someone cleared her throat.

He spun around to see Grams on the stairs with a pile of blankets in her arms.

Sam sighed and stepped away from Robin. He took the blankets and spread them out on the couch. "Thanks, Mrs. Ingram. I'm wiped out. Three days of sleeping in the jail wasn't good for me."

"Can't be good for anyone." Grams frowned at Robin. "What's got you all het up?"

Sam felt his eyebrows rise. Hadn't she seen what he'd been doing? He looked at Robin's face and understood. He'd been thinking of kissing her, but she'd needed comfort, that was all.

Later, boy. It'll all come out later.

Robin's eyes widened as she stared at her grandmother. "You're kidding, right? Everything!"

Grams shrugged. "It'll all work out. It always does. I'm more worried about this young man sleeping down here where I can't hear what he gets up to."

Sam smirked but bent his head to hide it from the women. So she had seen what he'd been doing.

Grams stalked upstairs after a particularly meaningful glare at the two of them.

After she disappeared into the upper hallway, Robin laughed, a short bark that Sam had never heard from her before. "Well, she knows I'm human." She looked Sam up and down. "Or at least she knows you are. But then, why would she think you'd be interested in me?"

"Don't go there, babe." He gave her a measuring look and decided she was more exhausted than he was. "I really meant it when I said I was wiped out. How about we go over our plans in the morning?"

That made her smile. "OK. If you promise not to leave me out, that's OK."

"Never. I'll never leave you out." He tried to put as much feeling into the words as he could manage. *Just let Donovan make the wrong move, let us catch him, and I'll never leave her side. Please God. Please.*

The phone rang and Robin leaned across the couch to pick up the handset.

Mrs. Wright's voice, shaking, terrified, came over, loud enough for Sam to hear. "Where's Sam? You better find him and get Kerry back."

"What? What are you talking about?" Robin turned toward Sam, her eyes wide and shocked.

"You know what! Kerry's gone."

16

It was time. Everything had come together, matched up, made the perfect pattern, and the tapestry said it was time for him to finally take Robin, make her perfect, fix her. Look at the way she'd bumped up against him tonight, shifted closer to him, the sultry looks she'd given him, the fear when she'd looked at Sam.

It was time.

And here was the last thread he needed—the kid, Kerry. All it had taken was a few words of reassurance. After everything they all said to the kid, trying to keep him safe, and all it took was a word or two, and everything was in place. Robin adored the kid, for whatever reason. He'd make them both over, in *his* image, to his design, and she'd love to see them all in her last picture.

It was time to make Robin perfect.

❧❧

Becca lay down on her mattress with one hand under her cheek. With the other she scraped the broken end of her toothbrush against the crumbling hole in the wall. Jake knelt next to her and brushed the dust toward the end of the bed and covered as much of the hole as he could with her crumpled sheets.

"There's too much wood," Becca complained. "It's

all sticks."

Jake pushed her out of the way and prodded the wood with his fingers. "This could be good. We can maybe break them if we can expose enough of it."

Becca didn't understand what he meant, but she understood the word "good." She pushed her pillow against the wall and leaned on it, her thumb in her mouth.

They both heard fumbling at the door. Jake was quick. He shoved the sheets up and flew across the room to his own mattress, where he sprawled, just as the door opened and Mr. Bird pushed someone else inside.

The new kid wasn't much taller than Jake, but his face looked older. It looked funny, somehow, but Becca liked it. He limped in, shrugging his shoulders like he didn't want Mr. Bird to touch him. And he was crying.

"Why you doing this to me? I thought you were my friend!"

Jake stood up and moved closer to the boy.

Becca wanted to, too, but she was too scared of Mr. Bird. He might yell at her for being nice to the kid, or he might find the hole.

Mr. Bird glared at Jake. "Back off. He's not going to be here long."

"What are you gonna do to me?" The new boy wiped his face, and snot smeared across his upper lip. "I wanna go back to my mom. You said I could. You lied!"

"He lies to everybody," Jake said.

Mr. Bird's arm flew out, and he slapped Jake across the face, so hard that Jake fell. He put his hands over his head and lay on the concrete floor. Mr. Bird kicked him, not hard, but like he wanted Jake to get out of the way. It made the new boy cry out and shrink away from Mr. Bird. Mr. Bird ignored that, just pushed him toward Becca's mattress. "You can sit down over there, next to Becca."

The new boy stumbled under Mr. Bird's hand and shuffled a little closer to Becca. He looked like he didn't want to sit next to her any more than she wanted him to. What if he found the hole? But he wouldn't tell Mr. Bird, would he? Not when Mr. Bird was being so mean to him.

After a minute Jake pushed himself up, and he glared up at Mr. Bird. "It's true. Look how you lied to Becca. She thought you were a good guy."

"Shut up, or I'll shut you up myself." Mr. Bird grabbed Jake's shirt and jerked him up. Some of the buttons ripped off when he threw Jake back on his mattress, and his dirty shirt gaped open over his chest. "Shut up and you might get lucky."

Becca's thumb made those slurpy sounds everyone hated, and she tried to make herself be quiet, but she was too scared. She had to suck, hard.

Mr. Bird looked at her, and she shrank back against the wall. She hoped she was in front of the hole. He was mad enough already, and she didn't want him to throw her like he'd thrown Jake. She didn't want him to throw Jake again, either. Or do something worse. When she thought about what Mr. Bird might do to them for making that bad hole, her eyes got watery, and she sniffled.

Mr. Bird took a deep breath. When he smiled, Becca wanted to run away. She wanted her mom, right now, to take care of her.

"This is Kerry," Mr. Bird said. "He's going to be here for a couple hours, that's all. And after that, we're going to do your hair. OK? You're going to be ready for me, aren't you?"

Becca nodded. Her stomach wanted to throw up, but since Mr. Bird had forgotten breakfast again, and lunch, too, there wasn't anything to come up. Still, it was hard to swallow the sour in the back of her throat.

"Hey, don't look so scared. I brought you guys some dinner." He moved back to the door, slammed it, and a minute later came back with a plastic bag.

For once it wasn't sandwiches. Jake grabbed both thick white boxes, and he handed one to Becca. His expression told her not to move off the mattress. He sat next to her, and they dug into the spaghetti with their fingers. Becca looked sideways at Jake. One whole side of his face was red where Mr. Bird had hit him.

The new kid pointed at the boxes. "You told Robin you were gonna eat that. I heard you."

With his mouth full, Jake said, "He lied. Just like he lies all the time."

Mr. Bird took a step toward Jake. "I told you to shut up, kid."

"Why should I?" Jake let his almost empty box tumble to the floor as he jumped up. "You don't even know what my name is. You just want to kill me, like you killed Lehanie and Simon. Like you're gonna kill Becca and this kid."

Mr. Bird's eyebrows went up and his eyes were wide. "I'm going to *fix* Kerry." He made it sound like it was a good thing. Becca used to believe when Mr. Bird said good things about what he did, but not anymore.

Kerry glowered. "I'm not broke."

Mr. Bird laughed. "Look at your leg, Kerry, and your arm. Don't you want them to work right?"

Becca looked at Kerry. His right arm curled up

toward his chest, and it looked skinnier than his other one. His right leg looked smaller, too. He had a funny shoe on, with a really thick bottom, and poles stuck in it. The tops of the poles disappeared under his loose sweat pants. Maybe it was his shoes that made him limp a little.

Kerry looked like he might start crying again. "They work OK."

"Not as well as this kid's." Mr. Bird pointed at Jake. "Don't you want to be able to walk like him?"

Jake got even closer to Mr. Bird and Kerry. Maybe he wanted Mr. Bird to hit him again. He sure acted like it. It scared Becca to watch him. "What are you gonna do? Kill me and take my leg and my arm and sew it onto him? You gonna make a Frankenstein?"

This time when Mr. Bird hit him, Jake didn't get back up. Instead, he lay on the concrete floor and shook.

Becca thought he was crying. She wanted to go to him, but she didn't. She remembered. The most important thing was to hide the hole from Mr. Bird. But it was really hard to see Jake cry.

"Anyway, Kerry." Mr. Bird patted Kerry's shoulder, and his voice changed, went nice like he used to talk to Becca, like he still did, when he was talking about her hair. "I'm going to fix you. I'm going to make you perfect. You'll be just as smart as everyone else—"

"I already am!" Kerry shouted. His voice echoed off the concrete walls.

Mr. Bird put his arm around Kerry's shoulder. "Naw, but you will be. Don't worry. After I fix you, I'm going to fix these kids, and I'm going to fix Robin."

"Robin has bad legs." Kerry looked up, and big

tears rolled down his face. "She has other stuff too, but she's my friend. I like her the way she is."

"Yeah, but I'm going to fix her." Mr. Bird laughed. He looked like he didn't even see them anymore. Like he couldn't see how Kerry was crying, or Jake cringing on the floor, or how Becca was trying to hide the hole in the wall. Like he wasn't Mr. Bird anymore. Like he'd never been Mr. Bird at all.

☙❧

Robin paced the living room as well as a person on crutches could. Three steps toward the front door, shove a cushion out of her way, three steps back to the kitchen doorway.

Her grandmother sat at the kitchen table, the old, overhead light spilling a square of yellow across the table and her gray hair. She bent over her Bible, eyes closed, hands clasped.

Robin turned around. She didn't want to disturb her grandmother's prayer. She ought to be praying herself. But the tension in her limbs threatened to shake her apart, and she couldn't settle herself enough to concentrate. Every step was a *please, God*, every turn was a desperate attempt to escape thoughts of what might be happening to Kerry.

The killer *couldn't* kill Kerry. Whoever the killer was, Donovan or Danny, he *knew* him.

It wasn't Danny. Danny loved his team.

Donovan?

It didn't matter. The killer could, and would, do anything horrible. He'd already proved that.

And now Sam was out there, without sanction of the police, without someone to vouch for where he was, searching just as hard as everyone else, and under suspicion, as well.

Macias had already cleared him for this kidnapping, but who, outside of the police themselves, would know?

"Robin." Grams' gentle hands massaged her shoulders. "God's got it in control."

"I know. I just think we need to remind Him how much we love Kerry. How much we need him." She finally was able to sit on the edge of the couch and rest her crutches next to her. "Grams, why? Kerry has never done anything to anybody."

"You think those other kids did?"

"No. That's not what I mean." Robin hung her head. "I just wish everyone was safe."

"Don't we all?" Grams picked up her Bible and held it to her chest. "I'm heading up to bed. You going to try to sleep?"

"I don't think I can."

Grams shrugged. "You should try, anyway. Pray if you can't. And call me if you need me."

"All right." Robin looked up. "Thanks, Grams."

"Anytime, kiddo." Her grandmother made her way up the stairs, pulling herself one step at a time, and the usual guilt shook Robin. Grams was getting old and having to climb the stairs so many times a day didn't do her knees any good. If Robin were whole, if her legs worked right, she'd be the one using the upstairs bedroom, and Grams would be down here where it was easier.

But that wasn't Robin's fault or choice. Bemoaning it didn't help her grandmother. Robin was just trying to distract herself and making herself feel worse instead.

And she didn't know where Sam was.

He'd run out when Mrs. Wright called, saying something about Donovan's house. When Detective Macias showed up a few minutes later, Robin and Grams were able to give him Sam's alibi, but he scoffed when Robin told him Sam's theory.

"Donovan's got alibis," he'd said. Then he'd left, calling into his radio that the suspect was cleared and to start a city-wide search for Kerry.

He'd left Robin with no idea what anyone was doing, where Sam was, how much trouble he was in. She leaned back and closed her eyes. Grams puttering around her room, and the creak of her bed springs, were the only sounds Robin heard inside the house. Outside, the wind rustled in the leaves, and whined around the eaves. Perfect Halloween weather, only a week away, but who was going to let their children go out that night?

She sank onto the couch and clasped a pillow to her chest, shoulders shaking, holding in the tears so Grams wouldn't have to come back down.

&oc&

Donovan checked the lock on the storeroom door twice, and found himself going back to it again. *No. Don't do that. That's giving in to the demons. Letting them control you again. Don't do it. You have a job to do.*

And he'd better get started.

What had he planned for Kerry? He walked to pull aside one of the front curtains, peered out, let it drop. Kerry. What about Kerry?

He needed fixing. Jake had an interesting idea, using his limbs to fix Kerry's. Too bad he knew that was just a story, not something real. Although they managed organ transplants...

Donovan shook his head. No. He had to concentrate on the job he had to do. Set up the new picture. Get the cameras to Robin's house. Get the kids there. How was he going to do that?

Better to get Robin up to his house.

He paced to the kitchen and back to the living room, where he picked up one of the stuffed mermaids. She loved fantasy. She loved pretty things. She created pretty things, just like he did. She didn't know all they had in common.

But everything came clear. She didn't understand. Yet. She would, as soon as he explained. She'd understand, and she'd finally get how she needed to cooperate to make everything perfect.

He just needed to explain.

∂∘⋖

After he fetched his half-charged cell phone from home, not even checking the lock on the door he slammed behind him, Sam trudged up the hill. He kept his face bent against the wind, peering at the roadway in the dark. He heard voices calling, first one person clearing one area, then another just a few houses away, but he saw no one. The police probably had to wait for search warrants on any home they thought likely, but they wouldn't go after Donovan.

Macias had made that clear.

So it was up to Sam.

He trotted up several streets, slowing slightly as the incline steepened and he reached the farther limits of the town. He couldn't be this out of shape, not even after three days sitting in the jail, only able to do pushups and sedentary exercises. Fatigue and fear, pure and simple, stole his breath. He stopped a moment, closed his eyes, and asked God to guide him, help him, hold him up. Renewed, he started once again to run.

Beyond the last line of homes and hotels lay only chaparral scrub, and he'd searched there too many times already. He didn't believe anyone would find Kerry out in the brush. He was somewhere close to Donovan's house. Sam was sure.

Robin had given Sam Donovan's address, along with his phone number, which she'd gotten from the paperwork at the co-op. He lived in one of the houses farthest from the harbor—not a big seller if you were looking at real estate values, but when you wanted a convenient place to hide something—or someone—away, perfect.

Donovan was all about perfect.

It was a typical, narrow, two-story house, tired white in the frail streetlights and mist, and a bit run down. The grass had gone brown and sere, and weeds rather than flowers filled the beds in the front. The downstairs lights were on, and through one window, Sam saw the flicker of blue.

He edged between Donovan's house and the one just to the north. Neither had a backyard, just a narrow track between the buildings and a concrete retaining wall that held back a fall of rocks and the stubby wilderness that characterized Catalina Island. He prayed the neighbors didn't have a dog.

Few houses on the island originally had garages, but Donovan's had something like one slapped onto the side. A windowless room, maybe eight feet by ten, was wedged between the retaining wall and what Sam thought must be the kitchen. It had no outside entrance.

Perfect if you wanted to imprison a couple of kids.

He walked around the room, studying the foundation. It had no crawl space. The plaster and lathe walls seemed to grow from the bare dirt. He wasn't going to get inside from where he was. He'd have to go through the house.

But first he had to get Donovan out.

He had few options. He might make a disturbance outside, but not only would that likely bring the neighbors, it would only last a few minutes.

He pulled out his cell phone and called up Donovan's number.

"Hello?"

He took a breath for clarity. He had to play this right. He wasn't going to get another chance. "Hey, Donovan. It's Sam. Wanted to know if you'd heard the news?"

"I know you're out. You told me a couple hours ago."

"That, right. No, that's not what I'm talking about. I meant about Kerry."

"What about him?" But there was enough hesitation in Donovan's voice, and something else—a sort of satisfaction—that let Sam know he'd called the right man.

"He went missing. Remember he was at the restaurant?"

"Sure."

"They went home, each one doing their own thing, and when his mom went to tell him it was time for him to go to bed, he wasn't there."

"Wow. That's too bad."

The guy was losing his touch if that was all the sympathy he could manufacture.

"So we're all out looking for him."

"Yeah?"

"He can't be out all night. He doesn't have the stamina to hold up to a night out in the open." Or in Donovan's clutches, for that matter. "Anyway, Danny wants you to help with the search."

"Oh, sure. Tomorrow."

"He wants you tonight."

Silence answered at first. Then Donovan said, "OK, but I got a couple things to take care of. Maybe half an hour. You let Danny know for me, all right?"

"He needs you right now. Do you know how cold it is out here? Someone like Kerry couldn't stand the exposure for more than a few minutes, and it's been almost an hour already."

Another pause before Donovan ground out, "Ten minutes. Let him know."

"Sure thing."

That would give Sam time to scout up the hill for a good vantage point. He prayed that Donovan wouldn't touch the kids—that those ten minutes of grace wouldn't be long enough to hurt, or kill.

17

Becca watched as snot and tears rolled down Kerry's cheeks and upper lip. She sighed and went into the bathroom to grab a handful of toilet tissue. She took it back to him. Why didn't Jake take care of him? He'd always done that kind of stuff for Becca. But maybe, now they had a new kid, it was her turn.

She shook her head. She probably should take care of Jake, too. He still hadn't gotten up since Mr. Bird hit him.

She held the toilet tissue out to the new kid. "Here. You better wipe your nose."

He did, getting the worst of it off his face, and pushed the mess back at her. She made a face but took it.

"I saw you on TV. Your pictures. They had pictures from school and stuff." Kerry pointed first at Becca and then at Jake. "And a couple other kids. A baby. They found her, but not her babysitter. I mean, she was dead. There were some other people dead. Somebody killed them."

Becca stared up at him, and could barely ask, "Who killed them?" Maybe he'd say it wasn't Mr. Bird.

Kerry shrugged. "I dunno. First they said Sam did it, but he said no. And Robin said it wasn't Sam, and I believe her. She said I could trust Sam. So I don't know who it was. But it's a bad guy. I think it's Donovan." His eyes went wide, and he sniffled again. He looked around the room, dim now with only a faint light from the bathroom. "How'd you guys get here, anyway? Did Donovan bring you?"

Becca swallowed. "Mr. Bird brought us here."

"Who's he?" Kerry swayed and moved so his feet were farther apart, like he wanted to ride a bike. The bottoms of his pant legs came up and showed the poles, and some plastic bits that held them close to his leg.

"Mr. Bird." Becca pushed her hands at the door to show the new kid and tried to keep her chin from shaking. "He scares me. He used to be nice."

"Who's Mr. Bird? I'm talking about Donovan. That's Donovan." He jerked his hand toward the door. "The man who put me in here. The one who hit that kid." He pointed at Jake, still on the floor.

Becca squatted next to Jake. Red pooled under his nose. She used a corner of tissue that looked the cleanest to wipe at it. Jake rolled from his stomach to his side, peering up from under his arm at Becca. She smiled and patted his shoulder and looked up at Kerry.

"That was Mr. Bird brought you here. Maybe you only know his first name."

Kerry shuddered. "I don't want him to be the bad guy. He told me he wasn't. He said Sam was. Only Robin said he wasn't. But she didn't say anything about Donovan being the bad guy." He wiped more tears off his face with his sleeve. "I wish she told me. I get confused. She knows I get confused. She should've told me." He started to cry harder. "She told me not to trust anyone but Mom and Dad. She told me, and I forgot! She knows I forget stuff. She should have told me more."

Jake pushed against the floor and sat up. Blood

made another trail from a cut on his cheek to the corner of his mouth. Becca threw Kerry's tissues into the corner, washed her hands in the bathroom and wiped them on her pants. She got clean tissue and gave that to Jake. After that, she got more clean tissue for Kerry. As she handed the wad to him, she felt something good bubble inside her, like she was getting to be a big girl. Mommy always said she'd grow up. It looked like she had been, even without Mommy and Daddy to help her.

But they were there with her, anyway. Right in her middle where she kept them.

Jake wiped the blood and smeared it almost as much as Kerry had smeared the gunk on his face. When he threw the dirty tissue in the corner, he looked like he wanted to fight someone. The look in his eyes scared her as much as Mr. Bird did. Jake wasn't in his eyes anymore. He'd already gone off to fight whoever it was he hated, even though he started talking.

"He's going to kill all of us. And then he's going to kill that other one. The one he called Robin." His voice sounded like he'd put a paper towel roll to his mouth, and talked through that.

"He can't!" Kerry wailed. He wobbled again and backed up until he leaned against the wall. "He can't kill her. He likes her." His shoulders shook, and he wiped at his face again.

Becca got close enough to pat his shoulder, and he gulped.

"He takes pictures of Robin all the time, and he puts them all over his house. He told me. I even saw some of them. I saw them when he brought me here." He put his head back, almost yelling now. "He even gave me one. Robin saw it, and I told her he gave it to me. And she didn't say anything."

"Stop crying." Jake limped closer to Kerry. He walked as bad as Kerry had when he first stumbled inside the room. "It's gonna be OK. Just ask Becca." He laughed and shook his head like he had something in his ears, and pointed. "What's that thing on your leg?"

Kerry turned pink and looked down, not at his leg, but as though Jake had made fun of him and it scared him. "It's a brace."

"What's it for?"

Kerry frowned. "It's to make my leg strong. 'Cuz it's not strong all by itself. It's like my arm, only it has to help me walk. So it needs a brace."

"What's it made of?"

Becca picked up the empty food containers and dropped them in the pile on the corner. When they fell, some other things that were already on the pile moved and a nasty smell came up. She pinched her nose and turned her back on the trash.

"I don't know," Kerry answered Jake. "It's a brace." He rubbed his good hand over his bad arm, circled round and round his elbow with his fingers.

"Can I see it? Do you know how to take it off?"

"Why?" Now Kerry edged away from Jake and his staring, crossing his bad leg behind the other one.

Becca frowned at Jake, but he ignored her. "Look, Becca, show him the hole. Show him."

"Why?"

"Just show him." Jake turned back to Kerry. "You can't tell him about it, OK? That—what did you call him? Donovan? You can't tell Donovan what we're doing or anything."

Kerry nodded. "I won't tell him *anything*. He's bad."

Becca nodded, hard.

"Good." Jake hunkered in front of Kerry, not close, but like he wanted to rest. "So it's OK to show him, Becca." He sounded very tired.

Becca climbed onto her mattress and pulled the sheets away from the wall. The hole was bigger than a basketball now, except for some of the wood pieces that still stretched across it.

"We're trying to dig a hole so we can get out." She kneeled next to it. "We used our fingernails, and our toothbrushes, but those broke." She looked up at Kerry. "I know what Jake means! Maybe we can use your brace to dig. Then we can get out and Mr. Bird won't be able to hurt us."

Kerry frowned at her for a long time. Jake straightened next to him, looking like he wanted to jump on him and take the brace off all by himself. Finally, Kerry nodded. "OK." He sat down, his arms going in circles before he caught his balance. As soon as he had his balance, he pulled up the stretchy bottom of his sweatpants. "OK, there's buckles. I'm not good at buckles yet. Can you do them?"

"Yeah, I sure can." Jake kneeled in front of Kerry, and his hands were like Becca's daddy's, when she scraped her knee, soft and gentle. Becca could tell Jake wanted to be especially nice to Kerry. She was glad. She liked Kerry.

Jake pulled apart the buckles, and lifted the brace off of Kerry's leg.

"Will you look at that?" All three of them stared at the metal poles that stretched between the part that cupped Kerry's knee, and the part that strapped around his foot. "Metal. Kerry, I think you just saved all our lives."

❦

Twenty minutes later, Sam watched Donovan leave his house. He turned and spent at least a minute fumbling at the locks before sauntering toward the street. Sam edged down the hill as soon as Donovan disappeared.

Cactus and other spiny plants gripped Sam's jeans with tiny thorns, which broke as he slid past. Sam waited at the corner of the house, pressed flat against the wall, listening. He heard Donovan's footsteps and when the sound faded to almost nothing, he rounded the side of the house.

How could Donovan not suspect him? How could he walk away from the house and the kids, as though they were hidden from every eye?

Well, two possibilities. Either the kids were secreted somewhere else, or Donovan was not the kidnapper.

And Sam didn't believe either of those solutions.

So it must just be a case of supreme confidence on Donovan's part. *Please, God, don't let him remember he's forgotten something and come back. Please, let me find the kids. Don't let me let them down.*

Donovan had left the porch light off, which made messing with the lock a bit of a problem. And there wasn't just one lock, but three. A simple key lock and two inside bolts. They looked to be of different manufacturers, and for sure Sam had no clue how to break in.

From there, he went around the side of the house to check the windows.

Most were boarded up. Those that weren't, were

barred. Had the cops even come to check out his house? Each defense added more evidence to Sam's theories, but as he was already positive, he didn't need the proof. He just needed a way inside. Because he was sure those kids were there, and they were in terrible danger.

He called Robin on his cell. "I got him to leave, but I can't get in the house. You think you could convince Macias to send some men out here to check it out?"

"I'll try." She sounded like she didn't believe she'd have any effect on the detective, and Sam had to agree with that. Macias was so sure Sam was wrong.

"Try Bricker."

"He lied about you!" Her righteous indignation on his behalf warmed something inside him and made him wish this was all behind him. That they were together, over the horror, and working on a new phase to their relationship.

Soon. He would be with her soon.

For now, he had to concentrate on getting the kids out of the house. "Actually, no, Bricker didn't lie." Sam leaned against the wall and dug through his pockets. Nothing huge and heavy like a forgotten Maglite. Not that he'd forget a monstrous flashlight, or anything else useful. Not until he was going to need it, anyway. He pulled out the penlight clipped to his keys. "That was all Macias. He wanted to arrest me, so he rearranged a bit of evidence to suit him."

"In other words, the lead detective is the one who lied." More anger threaded her voice.

"Well, yeah. But he had his reasons, babe. Look, I'm going to keep trying to find a way inside. You make some calls, all right?"

"I will."

"And Robin?"

"Yeah?"

He let the pause build just a fraction of an instant. "I love you."

"Oh, Sam." A choked moment passed. "I love you, too. Be safe!"

"I plan to, but I'm more interested in getting those kids out of this house."

He hung up and pocketed his cell. If he had a car, he could use it like a bulldozer. A golf cart wouldn't have the same stellar results, and besides, he didn't want to take the time to hike down to Robin's to fetch hers.

He started yet another trek round the house.

∂∞∞

Now that he understood what he was meant to do, everything else faded away. It was just him and Robin. They were the only ones who mattered. The kids, Sam, all the people surrounding Robin and trying to interfere—none of them mattered. Now he knew what he had to do. He had to convince Robin.

He had to get to her, show her what he meant. He could fix her then.

He knew just how he'd pose her. Had it all figured out, from the first time. The first girl—Lehanie. Robin would be dancing just the same way. Maybe have a butterfly fluttering around her hair. That would be a nice touch. No kids, no one else. Just Robin and Donovan.

His camera had a timer, he could pose her, and put himself into position for each shot.

But he'd forgotten his camera. He had to go back

now.

He turned around, stopped, and laughed out loud. The cops would take plenty of pictures. He didn't have to worry about it. He had everything he needed to fix Robin in his pockets.

Robin and himself.

Because sometimes, he forgot what the whole plan was about. He forgot how everything was meant to be about him and Robin, that Sam had never had any part in it. That had been his mistake before. He'd put Sam in the picture.

Of course, that had all worked out, because it gave the cops even more of a reason to look at Sam. That, and the way he found the baby within minutes of Donovan dropping her off. Sam had almost caught him then, almost ruined the plan, but that had worked out, too. Donovan was glad. He wouldn't want a baby's death on his conscience.

Now everything had worked out again. Everyone would be out looking for Kerry. Especially Sam. Robin couldn't search, so she'd be home praying. Alone. Maybe her grandmother would be there. Donovan frowned. But she was old, she couldn't do anything to stop the plans.

Yes. Everything had worked out right. The plan was back on track. He'd have Robin, the kidnappings and killings would stop, just like she'd been praying for, so she'd be happy.

Oh, yes. God must be smiling.

꙰ꙮ꙰

Robin hung up and dialed the detective's number. It went to voicemail.

"Sam is up at Donovan's, and he says it looks suspicious. He's sure the kids are there—all three of them, and he wants you to send some men out there. Now. Please." She added the last, and wondered if it would sound as wimpy to him as it did to her.

Bricker's number gave her the same option. She left Donovan's address that time, but didn't have any more hope. After speaking to the police dispatcher, who promised to contact "all officers involved," she dialed Sam. His phone went to voicemail as well. "No one answers tonight. Not even you. I don't think they'll show up to help but I left messages. Oh, Sam, I'm scared!"

After she hung up, she wished she hadn't mentioned her fear. He didn't need to worry about her on top of everything else.

This waiting would drive her nuts. She'd experienced plenty of times in her life where she longed to have working-order legs, longed to be able to do what everyone else did with so much ease, with so little thought. Tonight, though, that longing twisted inside and left her almost in tears. She couldn't go after Kerry. She couldn't do a thing to back up Sam. She could sit in her room, safe in her own little house, and worry. That's all she was good for.

Except prayer.

Prayer. Probably the best thing she could do. And not just her, not just gimpy Robin, but anybody—the best thing anyone could do.

She'd just reached for her Bible when a rustle outside her window made her jump and turn. Something flickered beyond the curtains of blue beads and was gone. Why would Sam come to the window rather than the front door? She'd given him a key. Why would anyone?

She crawled off her bed, fitted her crutches over her hands, turned off the light next to her bed, and limped to the window. The beads stirred as she brushed them away, clacking and shushing as they slid around her shoulders.

She put her face to the glass, peering into the darkness.

Another face grinned back, and she screamed.

🙠🙢

"I can't walk without my brace," Kerry said. "Don't break it, 'K?"

Jake looked up, his brows wrinkled in concentration. "I'll try. It's not plastic, so it'll hold up better than all the stuff we broke. But we have to get out. You get that, right?" His hand tightened on the metal pole. "If we don't get out, that guy is gonna kill all three of us and go after Robin." He shoved the end of the brace back into the hole. "And then it won't matter if you can walk or not."

"Yeah." Kerry's face crumpled, and Becca knelt next to him and patted his shoulder. She'd never met someone bigger than her who cried more. But she still liked him.

"Mr. Bird talked about Robin all the time," she said. Kerry just turned to look at her. "He really likes her. He said she has black feathers and pretty blue eyes. I never knew a bird who had blue eyes."

Kerry laughed. "Not feathers, silly. She's not a bird. She's a person. She has black hair. It's real long and when we play baseball she has to put it in her hat, or tie it up."

"Does Mr. Bird play baseball with you?"

"No. He watches and takes pictures." He leaned forward to see what Jake was doing. "That's a big hole."

"Yeah, and we don't want him to know it's here. So we hide it. Don't tell him if he comes back, OK?"

"'K." Kerry scooted off the mattress and crawled, like a crab on its back, toward Becca's mattress. "Can I help?"

"You are helping. You're letting me use this." Jake sat back, panting, and waved the brace. Already the end of it was covered with white dust. "I'm making the hole really big, all the way through to the outside, and then I'm gonna try to break some of the wood with this."

After that, Becca and Kerry didn't talk much. Neither did Jake, although he grunted a lot every time he shoved the pole of the brace between the strips of wood and pulled. After a couple minutes, one piece of wood cracked, splintered, and fell onto Becca's pillow. Jake shouted, not with any words, but with triumph, and jammed the pole in again. The next board broke, and the brace pole came away bent.

Becca glanced at Kerry. He frowned hard at Jake, but he didn't say anything.

After the third strip of wood broke, Jake turned the brace around and jammed it into the outside of the wall.

It took a lot longer than Becca thought it had to. She started to count, first in her head, but it wasn't enough and she had to count out loud. And when she got to six and couldn't remember how to go any higher, Kerry kept on counting for her.

He got up to twenty-two when Jake let out another

shout. After that, things got crazy. Jake threw the bent up brace behind him and got right down on the floor. He punched at the wall, and for the first time in weeks, Becca smelled outside air.

She wanted to put her face right up to it and breathe, because it smelled so much better than the trash and dirty bathroom smells from inside the room. There wasn't any sun, though. She'd missed the sun so much, and now it was still gone. Maybe Mr. Bird had made it go away forever.

"Hey!" Jake screamed, with his face right up to the hole. "Hey, we're in here! Let us out! The new kid's here, too, that Kerry! Let us out!" He stopped yelling and waited.

No one answered.

Jake jumped up. "Becca, you gotta squeeze through the hole and find someone to help us. I'll keep trying to break through the wall, but I can't fit right now. I think you can."

Becca dropped to her knees next to him. Now that she had to try to crawl through, the hole looked tiny.

Jake said, "I'm gonna hold the back of your head so nothing pulls your hair, OK?" He squatted next to her and put his hands on her shoulders. "You can do it, right? You can get out. And you gotta run as fast as you can and get somebody to come here. Don't call him Mr. Bird, either. Call him Donovan. No one out there knows who Mr. Bird is."

Something inside her chest kept banging. She was so scared. That was her heart, right? She'd never remember what Jake told her. But he didn't give her a chance to ask him to say it all over again, so she could get it right.

He pulled her toward the hole, and punched at the

wall a few more times. His hands were covered with white dust, mixed with blood. She didn't want to bleed to get out of the room, but maybe she had to. Maybe it was OK, anyway. After all, Jake was bleeding to get her out, wasn't he?

Just before she lay down to wriggle through, she remembered something. She grabbed Jake's face. "See? I *told* you God would get us out. I told you He'd send someone to help us. And He did! He sent us Kerry!"

Becca made herself as skinny as a snake, and stuck her head through the hole in the wall.

∂∞∂

Glass shattered and spilled over the sill. Some of it sparkled toward the floor, and Robin flailed back, nearly falling. She only caught herself up by grabbing onto the sewing table.

A second later Donovan jerked the window open.

Robin screamed again and stumbled away from him, whacking her legs with the crutches, trying to angle toward her bed, where her cell phone lay open.

"I don't think so." Donovan darted past her and snatched it up. After a quick check, he stuffed it in his pocket. "It's OK, though, Robin. You don't have to be scared. Sam called me and told me to come over." He nodded, smirking. Something in his ice blue eyes glowed, and she wondered that she'd never seen a hint of insanity before. Now she couldn't see anything else.

"He didn't call you. He wouldn't ask you to come here." Even fisted around her crutches, her hands tensed more. *God, help me, because I can't help myself.*

Donovan shook his head and moved closer. The frantic stare in his eyes changed to amusement, and something gentle that she would never again believe in. "Yeah, yeah. He did, really. He wants me to take care of you. Protect you from Danny. Coach Danny, remember? Remember we said he's the killer? And Sam wants me to get you fixed up." He reached out to run a hand along one strand of hair and set off a chain reaction of horrified chills. "That's what he said. He called me, just a little while ago. He said you're all worried over Kerry, and he's going after Danny to get him back, and you want me to fix everything."

All that talk of fixing. He'd mentioned fixing her before. How many times? And she'd never felt the alarms that filled her now, only anger. Why not? Why hadn't she seen? Why hadn't anyone else?

But she had to focus. "Where is Kerry?"

"He's safe. No, really. He's safe. Sam is going to get him from Danny." Donovan glanced toward the living room where the only light in the house glowed. "Your grandmother in there?"

Robin shook her head. "She heard me scream. She went for the cops."

"No, she didn't. I bet she's upstairs." Donovan chuckled. "That's gonna be pretty funny. She's gonna come down tomorrow and find you and me all fixed up. Perfect. She's gonna be really happy."

And what could she say? *Grams likes me just the way I am. I don't need to be fixed up. Whatever you do to me, she's not going to be happy about it*...but the words choked her, and they wouldn't make any more difference said that they did right now, silent in her mouth.

Donovan moved closer.

Robin scrambled away as far as she could until she felt the blankets with the backs of her knees. She wouldn't go any farther. She didn't want to end up on the bed in front of him.

He stroked her hair again and she pulled away, angrily, tossing her head like a skittish horse.

"You're so beautiful, Robin. We're going to be so beautiful together. I wish I could see the pictures. I always take pictures, you know." His voice went higher than normal, as though it, along with his sanity, had slipped away from him. His hands shook as he leaned close to Robin.

"Everyone knows you take pictures." But nausea filled the back of her throat. What kind of pictures was the man talking about? What kind would a maniac take and talk about with such love and pride?

Then she remembered Sam's descriptions of the first victim, how Lehanie had been posed, how, after they found Kaitlyn with crutches and more dyed black hair, everyone realized the killer had fixated on Robin.

And now she knew. If only someone had thought to look for pictures before now.

"Those aren't the pictures I'm talking about." He giggled and seemed to hear the irrationality in his voice and got a grip on himself. He shook his head, and his voice lowered an octave. "No one's ever going to see these. I can't post them in any gallery. I wish I could. I wish I could show them to you. I'd love to see your face when you looked at them." He swung his arm, his eyes alight again, and terrifying. "These are my special pictures. All kinds of my sweet, little Robins. Oh, and there was the one with Sam. Did you like that? You didn't see the pictures, though. Not the good ones. Maybe you saw the police ones, maybe Sam showed you those. You were so beautiful, dancing in the waves. I didn't think they'd pick on Sam for that one, but I'm glad they did. It gave me more time."

"You're sick." She flinched; sure he would retaliate for that remark.

But he only smiled. "You don't understand. Not yet. I'm a photographer. I like things to be perfect. Perfectly beautiful. Don't worry." Again, he reached for her. His hand, stroking her cheek, coming to rest on her shoulder, made bile rise in the back of her mouth. "When we're done, you're going to be all fixed up, and no one will ever think you're not perfect again."

She took a deep breath. "You're not going to touch me."

"You're just like Kerry. That was so funny. There you were telling him not to trust anyone. And you meant Danny, and he had no idea. No one did." His giggle surfaced for a moment before he repressed it again. "Now, it's just you and me. Just the two of us."

Had those ice blue eyes always been so unfocused?

"People are looking for him."

"Oh, sure they are. Sam is. He told me all about it. But they'll find him soon enough. You don't have to worry about Kerry."

Confusion drowned under new understanding. And she'd doubted Sam. "What about Becca and Jake?"

"Is that the kid's name? I kept forgetting." He shrugged. "He's a little punk anyway. Who cares what happens to him? He's not the kind of kid I'd ever want. Becca now, she's perfect, except for her hair." He frowned. "I never got time to fix her hair. That kid kept yelling at me, getting me all mixed up."

"You said Coach Danny had him."

Donovan giggled and shrugged again, giving her

an arch lift of his brows, as though he were as young as the children he'd taken. "You know where they are."

"No, I don't."

"Don't be silly. Sam figured it out, didn't he? You know why I'm here. It's nearly over. But it's been beautiful, hasn't it?"

His hand went to her throat.

Robin twisted away from him and stumbled. Her desk caught at her hip, digging in, but holding her upright. She used both crutches at once and took a giant swinging step toward the door.

Donovan blocked her, and his tackle sent her spinning toward the window. His arms around her protected her from the impact, but imprisoned her at the same time.

Screaming until her throat seared, she turned and raised a crutch, ready to bring it down on his head. Instead, the tip caught on the strings of beads, tangled and jerked to a stop, and never touched him. Only the beads, freed now from their strings, rained down on his grinning face.

18

Sam heard a yell, very faint, and far away. He wasn't sure where it came from, but he bolted around the corner for the third time and shone the beam of his flashlight across the outer walls of the tiny room. A sound made him stop.

Breathing. A child sobbing, but trying to hold it in, terrified.

He reached for his cell and punched in 9-1-1. "I think I found the missing kids."

"Stay on the line," the dispatcher said. "Where are you?"

"A few houses beyond the second bend on Stage Road. Donovan Haggart's house." He gave the address he had memorized. "I can hear one of them crying."

He went on playing the light over the wall—the window-less, door-less wall—at window height, at child height, seeing nothing, and yet hearing that heart-jerking, trying-to-stop sob.

"All our available officers are out now on the search."

"I know that. I'm helping. And I think—"

He stopped at the sound of a grunt and something breaking. Wood, or plaster, not a window, thank God.

And he realized what he'd forgotten.

Yes, thank You, God. Help me get them out of here, now.

"Sir?"

"They're here." He snapped the cell shut and shone the light near the ground.

A dirty, tangled mass of greasy curls that was not cactus or weeds made him hold the beam steady, and he dropped its angle. A crumpled face peered up at him from the very foundation of the house. Where there had been only flat plaster the first time he had checked, now opened a hole big enough—or almost big enough—for a five-year-old to squeeze through.

Sam crouched next to her. "Becca? It's OK, honey. I'm here to help you get out."

Her expression went from terrified, to relieved, to agonized, and even in the almost useless light, he saw her eyes fill with tears.

"You're going to be OK now, Becca. All right? I'm going to get you out, and you'll never have to go back in there."

She nodded, gulped. "You gonna get Jake and Kerry, too?"

"I sure am. But you first. Are you ready?"

"Yeah." She hitched up on her forearms and her eyes spilled over with tears. Her wail broke his heart. "I want my mommy!"

"You're going to see your mommy really soon. I promise." He lay on his stomach, his elbows holding him up.

"That's what *he* kept saying." Childish anger and betrayal broke his heart. "*He* kept promising she'd come get me, but she never did. Daddy either." She sobbed again and wiped at her nose with the back of a dirty hand.

Sam brushed some of the debris away from her hair and reached past her shoulder to grasp a broken splinter of lathe. "She's really going to come this time. You won't be able to keep her away from you. But right now, I need you to close your eyes. I have to break this wood off so you can get all the way out. I don't want anything to get in your eyes."

The wood came away with a crack, more plaster shivered over Becca's head, and the hole widened enough that nothing would snag her clothing. He grabbed her upper arms, their brittle delicacy sending another shaft of anger through him, and tugged. Becca put her head down and wriggled. Sam imagined her legs churning behind her.

"Is Jake pushing, too?"

"Yeah." Her breathy voice was weary. "I think I kicked him."

"You might have. Just stop moving." He shifted again, got his hands in a better position under her arms. "You've got to be just like Pooh Bear. Remember when Winnie the Pooh ate too much honey and Piglet pushed and Rabbit pulled, and he finally popped out?"

"Yeah?" Now her voice held a question and interest. Good.

"Well, you've got to do just what Pooh did, and let us do all the work now. Pretty soon you'll pop right out."

He felt the tension leave her shoulders. "'K."

She didn't exactly pop and fly out of the hole. But within seconds, Sam had eased her tiny body over the splintered wood and crumbling plaster, and he knelt in front of her, holding her gently in his shaking arms.

Becca was free.

Someone shouted from the hole. Sam didn't understand all the words, but he put his hand down to the opening. "Hey, it's Sam. Who's this? Jake?"

Kerry wouldn't be able to get down that close to the floor.

"Where's Becca? If you did anything to Becca..." The suspicion and menace in the kid's voice made Sam grin.

"She's right here. She's OK. Do you have enough room to get out?"

After a few more grunts, Jake said, "Almost. Kerry can't get out on his own. I broke his leg brace. He has to go first. I gotta help him."

"OK, that's fine. You help him while I try to make your hole bigger." Their excellent hole. Their excellent, brilliant, God-blessed hole. The words, and more, of praise, went through his mind, and he worked to pull away the wreckage. As he fought with the materials, the words came aloud. "Oh, God, thank You for these wonderful kids. Thank You that You made them so resourceful. You did great, Jake. You did such a great job. I am so proud of you. You know that?"

Pain ripped through his hands, and blood—his or the kids', he didn't know—made the plaster slippery, but within a few minutes Sam had made the hole big enough even for Kerry to crawl through without too much in the way of contortions. And when he saw Kerry's tousled head and heard his voice, sobbing now, he almost cried, not so much in sympathy as joy.

He reached down. "Kerry, buddy. It's Sam. I'm going to pull you out, OK? Just like I did with Becca."

"Sam?" The rumpled hair tipped back, and Sam saw Kerry's forehead, the tip of his chin as he struggled to squeeze close to the opening. "I can't see you."

"I know. It's OK, it's me, I promise. Donovan isn't here."

"He brought me here. He was mean, Sam. And you dinnit tell me he was bad. And Robin dinnit tell me, either. Why not?" Reproach that was pure Kerry laced his voice.

"We were scared. Here. Reach your arms out. Hey, Jake, can you push him from behind when I give you a yell?"

"Sure can."

Oh, but Sam liked the sound of the kid's voice. He glanced over his shoulder to where Becca stood just behind him. "You OK, kiddo? We're almost done here."

"I'm OK." She stuck her thumb in her mouth.

"But he almost got me," Kerry said. His voice rose in a whine.

"I know. We had to take that chance, Kerry. Anyway, we thought he liked you. We didn't think he'd hurt you."

"He did."

And he'd pay for that. God willing, the guy would pay for hurting an innocent like Kerry, or Becca or Jake. God willing, Sam would not have a hand in that. He didn't want that kind of act on his conscience.

"Hold my wrist. Can you do that? Right here." He guided Kerry's good hand to his left wrist and wrapped his fingers around. "Hold on as tight as you can. I'm going to pull you out. And it might hurt a little, Kerry. If it does, I'm so sorry. But it's better for you to be outside than in there."

"'K."

"Give me your other arm."

Kerry's twisted arm poked a few inches out of the hole. Sam grabbed his wrist, tightened his grip on Kerry's good arm, and pulled, slowly this time. Kerry was bigger, heavier, and nowhere as sturdy as the five-year-old. Once Kerry's shoulders passed the teeth of lathe poking from the hole, Sam called, "All right, Jake, push."

The extra strength got the young man out within seconds. Sam scrambled backwards, bent to lift Kerry, and set him on his feet. Only as Kerry toppled did he remember Jake's words about breaking the leg brace.

"Lean against the wall, OK?" He bent forward to whisper in Kerry's ear. "Hold Becca's hand, would you? She's still really scared. She needs you."

Kerry swallowed the sobs Sam could see building, straightened his shoulders, and reached for the little girl. "C'mere, Becca. Come over here while Sam gets Jake out."

Sam got back on his knees, suddenly aware of the pain in them, and called, "You ready to come out?"

"You bet."

Within seconds, Sam had hauled Jake out, and stood, looking at the three. "You guys are gonna be OK." He whispered the words, though he wanted to shout them.

This was the end. They'd catch Donovan, and no more kids would go missing. There wouldn't be any more ghastly corpses to find.

Sam dialed his phone again. "I've got the kids. I'm taking them out to the street. Send an ambulance, they look malnourished, and Jake is bleeding. Kerry's brace is broken, so he can't walk."

After dispatch promised to send help, Sam called Macias. "I sent Donovan out to help find Kerry. Find out who he's with and pick him up, because I just pulled Kerry and the other two out of his house."

"Stay right there."

Sam shook his head and turned to study the kids. "Come on. Let's go around to the front so they can see us from the street. The cops are going to come and maybe your parents. Or they might meet you at the hospital." He bent down in front of Becca. "Can you walk, honey?"

"I'll carry her." Jake wrapped his arms around her and tugged. Her feet hung almost to the ground before she wrapped them around his waist.

"I'll take her. She's too big for you."

Jake shook his head awkwardly around Becca's chin. "Nah. You gotta get Kerry. That's my fault, that his brace is broken."

"Is not," Kerry mumbled as Sam swung the young man up in his arms. "It's Donovan's. 'Cuz if he hadn't been the bad guy, you wouldn't't've had to break it."

Jake laughed, and over Becca's head, he met Sam's gaze.

The boy was a hero.

"You're awesome, Jake. I am so proud of you." He'd said it before, and he didn't feel he'd said it enough. "Of all three of you. You're" —What was Kerry's word? —"Awesome. You guys are absolutely awesome."

Jake started to shake his head, but Becca grabbed his cheeks. "He's right. The good guy is right, Jake. You're —you're —what he said."

"Awesome," Kerry told her. "Jake is awesome, just like me and Sam." After a second, he added, "An' you, Becca. You're awesome, too."

Sam looked down. "Kerry, my friend. Boy, am I glad to see you."

Kerry choked on a sob but finally he was able to say, "I'm glad to see you, too, Sam. I'm glad you're not the bad guy. That's Donovan, isn't it? Is Robin OK? He said he was gonna go get her, to fix her."

Sam froze.

ॐॐ

Blue and green beads cascaded across the floor, flowing like water, and Robin, off balance already with one crutch tangled in the strings, fell. Her shoulder glanced off her sewing table and the sewing machine toppled onto her. She threw up her arm and it slammed into her elbow before tumbling to the floorboards. An instant of alarm at seeing her most-used tool on its side, followed by another, more immediate, dose of terror, filled her.

Donovan laughed. "Good thing you're not going to need that anymore, isn't it? Come on, get up." He waved his hand at her.

"I can't." Robin rolled to her stomach and grabbed her crutch again. She could get up without help, if she had enough space, and if there weren't a thousand beads rolling around, but she didn't want him to know. Somehow, every fraction of information she could keep from him gave her a little more of an edge against him. Even if it was never near enough, she wanted it.

She gripped the middle of the crutch like a club and jammed it at the floor, pushing herself to her knees.

Donovan grabbed her around her middle and hauled her upright. "Aren't you excited? You're never going to have to do this again. No more struggling. No more not being able to walk. You're going to be perfect." His words huffed with the effort of carrying her weight.

She jerked her sore elbow back, and it collided with his stomach.

He grunted and laughed again. "Don't be silly. And stop fighting me. I'm going to help you."

"Let me go." She tried to wriggle out of his hold, but his arms tightened around her.

"Nope." He pulled her around, still with her back to him, and hauled her toward the living room.

"I'm going to set it all up right here. Right in the middle of the room. I forgot my camera, though. Stupid Sam. He sent me down here, and I came so fast, I forgot everything. It's all happening so fast now. But that's OK. It's time. They'll take pictures, anyway." He stilled. "Not that they'll ever be as good as one of mine."

Robin shook her head, her body limp with shock, and struggled again. Sam hadn't sent him. Donovan's mind was so far from reality he wouldn't be able to tell the truth if he tried.

Maybe he'd seen Sam, which was likely enough. Sam had gone to his house, after all, sure the kids were there.

But then, what had Donovan done to Sam?

Dare she ask?

"Where's Sam now?" The words came, forced out by fear and longing, words she never meant to say.

"All fixed up, Robin. Remember? I fixed him up. On the beach, remember?"

She closed her eyes. Did he mean Simon, whom he'd arranged to look like Sam, or was he talking about something he'd done tonight?

She sagged in his arms. Now she had nothing. Nothing to hold between herself and this monster, this depraved aberration who was so intent on killing her and calling it a good thing. Because if she didn't have Sam, if he'd killed Sam to get to her, what did she have?

God.

She had God.

Nothing but God. And that was enough.

God wouldn't want her to give up or give in to death. And so she wouldn't. Donovan might still win. He might succeed in setting up his gruesome display, and she would still die, but not with her consent.

Her crutches, caught against her sides, banged her legs. If she could get one free, she could try to hit him again. She wriggled harder, twisting her arms any way she could to break his hold.

"Stop it!" Donovan's hand shot out, clipping her under her jaw. Robin's head rolled, and mist went gray at the edges of her vision.

She might end up losing sooner than she'd expected.

19

Sam's heart refused to stop pounding, though he couldn't move.

Jake stopped on the edge of the street and set Becca on the ground. As he straightened, she kept her arms locked around his neck. He whispered something to her, and she nodded. She let him slide her down until she could lean against him, and stick her thumb in her mouth. Even in the dim light, Sam saw how much weight she'd lost since she'd posed for her kindergarten picture. Her face was pale and smeared, and both she and Jake probably hadn't bathed or changed clothes since they'd been taken.

Jake looked up at Sam. "He meant he's gonna kill her."

Finally, he could move. "I know." Sam fumbled for his cell phone, got it open. The dispatcher took note of Robin's address and said she would send officers out immediately. Her voice sounded calm and unruffled, standard issue, when he wanted her to scream in alarm and promise Robin would be all right, promise that no one on the force would let Donovan hurt her.

She couldn't. He knew that, but that didn't stop him wanting her to.

"He really is gonna kill her," Jake said. "You know her, right? He's got some crazy idea—I mean, he's *really* crazy—that killing her is gonna fix her."

"How do you know?" What had the idiot exposed these kids to? Had they *seen* the deaths or the bodies? And if they had, what kind of irreparable damage would they carry for the rest of their lives?

Thank God he'd socked Kerry away in that virtual dungeon, instead of exposing him to more of his filth.

"He told us. He said he was going to fix her like he fixed Lehanie and them. He's crazy." Jake, as thin and pale as Becca, with darkened bruises on his face, looked up at Sam. Several of the cuts still bled.

Sam set Kerry down but kept his arm around him. The young man clung to him, and pushed hard against his side. Sam resisted the urge to thrust him away and sprint down the road to rescue Robin. He shook his head. "When was this?"

"Right after he brought Kerry. A while ago. It took me a long time to make the hole big enough for Becca. And I broke Kerry's leg brace doing it. I bent it all up." Jake patted Kerry's arm. "I'm real sorry, but your brace saved our lives."

"That's OK. I'm glad we got saved." Kerry's voice veered from scared and weepy, and crept closer to his more cheerful self. "Sam and you saved us, Jake. You're both heroes. Did you know that, Jake? You're a hero, and you're just a little kid. That means you're awesome."

"Yeah. Right." Jake rolled his eyes. "What about this Robin? Are the police gonna get to her house in time?"

Sam saw the struggle the boy had, trying to keep the tears from filling his eyes. "I don't know. God willing, they will."

Becca pulled her thumb out of her mouth. "God will help." Her light, sweet voice sounded like a tract from a Sunday school class. "He helped us, and He sent Kerry to us so we could get out. He'll help the p'lice get to her and save her."

Sam knelt in front of the little girl and brushed dirty hair off a dirty cheek. "God did a great job saving you three, didn't He? We should thank Him."

"I did. Right when you pulled me out of the hole."

Oh, for the faith of a child. Sam wished he still had it. "Pray for Robin, honey. Pray hard."

Becca nodded. Her thumb slurped comfortably back into her mouth and her eyes squeezed shut.

Answer her, please, Sam begged. He turned to Jake. "Did he take anything with him when he left?"

Jake shrugged. "How should I know? I never got out of that room until just now. But he's had lots of time to get to her house. It only takes like ten minutes to walk from the beach up here, by that path he uses. That's how he got me and Simon up here."

His scout leader. Jake probably knew the man had died, but Sam didn't want to ask. If Jake didn't know, Sam sure didn't want to be the one to tell him.

A police siren broke over the edge of the hill, lights glowed like a sunrise. Soon the car roared up the bend and stopped beside them. Macias left the motor running and his door open. Before he could start asking questions, Sam said, "You've got to find Donovan. He's after Robin."

"I heard the call go out. No one's seen him." As if that made it less likely that he was stalking his real victim.

"He's gone after her. He told the kids he was going to get her."

"All right." Macias leaned inside the car for the radio and listened to the static. "Officers are already on their way to her house."

An ambulance pulled up behind his squad car, followed by three more police cars.

Sam's heart thudded as he saw the number of officers swarming the hillside. "They're all here."

Macias waved a hand, more interested in the kids. "Not all of them."

"Drive me down there." Sam grabbed Macias's arm.

"No one's taking a civilian into a dangerous situation."

Sam turned on him. "You used me," he ground out. "You put everyone in danger—Kerry, all the kids, Robin. Especially Robin. And now you're not even concerned? Take me down there now."

Bricker ambled over from another car. "I'll take him down."

After a moment of studying Sam's furious face, Macias nodded. "You'll just be in the way, but go ahead. Keep him out of the action, you hear?"

Bricker nodded. "I hear. Come on. Let's go."

৵৶

Some of the mist blinding her faded, and Robin turned her head to see Donovan frowning at her. His hand on her stinging cheek was gentle and made her tremble with horror.

"You'll get a bruise, Robin. You shouldn't do things that leave marks, you know. It's not good for the pictures." He straightened and glanced at the bed, then up at the ceiling, before he looked back at her.

"I didn't—" She stopped, fury mixing with revulsion. Her skin wanted to crawl away from his touch. He was not rational. How could she expect to reach him like a normal human? Yet, at the moment, he neither looked nor sounded insane. He'd slipped back into normal, and that made him more frightening than anything she'd ever experienced.

He shook his head. "Everything has to be perfect. You see that, don't you? If it's not, it hurts something. Me. It hurts something inside me." He sounded like a crime victim on a confessional talk show with his hand clasped to his chest.

"Hitting me hurts *me*," she said.

"No one wants you to get hurt. Sam doesn't. Kerry doesn't. I sure don't. But you already know that."

"Hurting Lehanie and the others—how can you justify that?" There she went again, expecting him to respond like a rational person.

"Robin, I didn't hurt them. I swear it. I fixed them all up, yeah, but you know how I feel about hurting people. Kids, especially. That's who you're worried about, right? Little Becca and the baby. There was a baby, you remember? And the scout guy the kid was so fussed about. Oh, and the kid. And Kerry." He smiled, looking so much like a fond uncle that she wanted to throw up.

Maybe if she did, it would make him leave her alone.

"I never laid a hand on those kids. I swear. I took care of Becca. I read her a bedtime story every single night, and she let me tuck her in bed, but I never hurt her." For half a second she saw a ray of sanity, as though he knew she would escape to tell the truth, but madness swallowed it. The sudden change in his tone of voice was like a whip across her back. "Don't you ever say I hurt them. You better believe me."

She shrank away and nodded.

"I didn't hurt them." He took a breath, seemed to fill himself with a dangerous calm, and nodded, once, sharply. "Promise me you'll tell them I didn't hurt anybody. That's important to me, all right?" He didn't wait for her to answer, not that she could have.

Rage and confusion filled her throat.

"Look at the mess you made with all these beads." He waved his hand at the floor, shaking his head. "They were so pretty, too. Almost perfect."

She really was beginning to hate that word. But now, with him calmer, she might be able to really fight, on her terms. She fit one hand into a crutch, backed up a step, and shifted the other to her right hand.

"No, Robin. You don't need those anymore. Remember? I'm going to fix you so you never have to use them again. Come on. Let's just leave them here." He reached for her crutches, and, when she shifted them out of his reach, he waved toward the bed. "I want you to lie down. In just a couple minutes, everything's going to be perfect. See? I have the stuff right here."

He fumbled at his chest and pulled a plastic bag out from an inner pocket. Robin thought she saw a syringe. "See? Won't leave any marks the camera can see. It'll be inside your elbow, one little needle prick, that's all, and your arm is going to be around me. Around my neck." Sweat broke out on his upper lip. "You're going to be hugging me, right? And our legs will be entwined, just as if yours were normal. Perfect. No one will be able to see the inside of your elbow, so it'll be perfect."

And I'll be dead. Robin took a breath that didn't want to fill her lungs. "What about you? You'll know it's there." And who was crazier, Donovan, or herself for trying to talk to him like a sane person?

"I'll be right there with you. There's enough here for both of us, I promise. I was going to have you dancing. Maybe we should both be dancing. Would you like that better?"

Robin's weight shifted. She staggered away from him. *God, is this what You want? Am I the sacrifice that will stop him from killing other people? Because if he dies with me, then everything is all right?*

But she didn't want to die.

20

On the short trip down the road, Sam gave Bricker the more pertinent details, the most important being what Donovan planned for Robin.

"They've got officers there now." Bricker pointed at the radio, which had been silent during the entire ride. "Got there before we started, OK? She'll be fine."

"He's out of his mind. Criminally insane." Sam scrubbed the top of his head, desperate to relieve the tension that told him jumping from the car and running across the scrub would get him to Robin faster.

"We knew that from the beginning."

"Yeah, well, now he's after Robin and that makes it—" Sam stopped, unwilling to finish. Said aloud, the words would have too much terrifying reality attached to them. "No one has any idea what he'll do. I doubt he does. He told the kids he was going to *fix* her." No way could he imbue that word with all the hatred he felt toward it and toward the man willing to kill Robin for some broken synapses in his brain.

God, help me. I know I'm supposed to love my brother, but I can't see him that way. If it comes to a choice between them, You know who I'm going to pick.

Bricker tapped the steering wheel. "I'd go faster if I could."

That didn't help.

The radio flared, and Sam thought he heard

Robin's name. He held up his hand, straining to understand the words, but nothing more came across.

"She's fine." Bricker sounded as if he wanted to make them both believe a lie.

Sam groaned and yanked on the door latch.

"It's locked." Bricker pulled into the tiny Avalon neighborhood and glanced at Sam. "She'll be fine."

Sam closed his eyes. *God, I can't help her. One more time I've let someone who needs me down. And this one is going to kill me, because she's my life.* And why had it taken him so long to admit that? He must have known for years. Every time he'd held her in his arms, waiting for her to swing her bat, waiting for her to start her run to first base, his heart had known.

One more corner and they were on Robin's street.

Several cruisers blocked his view of the house, and finally, Sam was able to give in to his impulse and bolt from the car. Within seconds an officer stopped him, hand on Sam's chest, the other arm spread to keep him from dodging around him.

"No. Let me by."

"It's a crime scene."

That floored Sam. Crime scene meant *crime*, and what besides murder...?

He stepped back, turned, and when the cop lowered his arms, he darted around him and ran through the front door.

•••

Donovan's smile put Robin into horror overload. She lifted her chin. She might die trying to save herself, but she wasn't going to give in. Her death was no guarantee of his. If she lived, the police would still know who they were after, finally. They would hunt him down, and he would never get the chance to hurt another human being again. She didn't have to die to ensure that happened, and she would not give in kindly or easily.

God, be with me now. I don't want to die.

She slipped her right hand out of the crutch cuff and slid it down the staff, gripping tight. With the other crutch, Robin pushed herself straight. The first, she still held short, and she dropped the one holding her up to be able to put both arms into the swing.

She'd practiced plenty on those swings, and her upper arm strength was phenomenal.

Donovan ducked away and stumbled on the beads, slid a few feet, and caught his balance. He backpedaled, his feet without purchase atop the tumbling beads, and his arms flailed.

She swung again. The crutch was a bat, Donovan, her target. She put every ounce of her strength into the swing, betting on a home run, betting on sending the ball out of the park. She had to think of it that way, and not as attacking another human being, or she would never be able to finish.

The metal pole collided with Donovan's head. Warm blood spattered her, her face and clothes and room, and he went down.

Robin tilted on her unsteady legs, fighting the urge to vomit, struggling to stay upright. She won the first battle, lost the second, and crumpled into a heap on her floor, amidst the rolling beads.

A muffled shriek came from the living room, and her grandmother rushed in. "Did I hear you scream?"

Robin lay her head down next to Donovan's unmoving body, uncertain whether to laugh or cry.

❧

Sam's rush stuttered to a stop just inside the front door. Robin lay in the doorway between her bedroom and the living room, her face splattered with blood, but alive, breathing. Grams came from the kitchen with a wet towel and handed it to her.

"Where is he?" Sam demanded. His chest heaved and rather than relief or thankfulness, his heart felt like lead. How could he have let this happen? How could he have let her down?

"In there. I hit him." Robin wiped the blood off her face and handed the towel back to her grandmother. Three officers filled up the living room, and one pointed into Robin's bedroom. Donovan lay amidst hundreds of beads, blood covering his face, groaning.

Defeated, far more than the man on the ground, Sam turned away, ready to let the officer throw him from the house, ready to walk away and let someone worthy of Robin find her and live for her. Because he hadn't. He hadn't saved her.

He heard his name, at first gentle, but it became more strident. He ignored Robin, ignored her grandmother, ignored all the words she was saying that he didn't want to hear. Either she knew the truth and berated him, or she didn't, and everything she said would be a lie.

Before he could finish turning away, a growl from Robin's bedroom made him look back. Grunting, Donovan rose from the floor. Blood mottled his face, streamed into his eyes and mouth. He held out his arms like a father running into a child's hug, and bellowed.

Bending his knees, Sam lunged. He caught Donovan in the chest, and broke his momentum. The two men stumbled over Robin's outstretched legs. Sam's hands slipped on Donovan's throat. He didn't know how they'd gotten there. He hadn't had any idea of strangling the man, but he couldn't let go.

As they went down on the living room rug, an officer got behind Donovan. Within seconds he had his hands cuffed, and was dragging him to his feet. The other two officers helped to haul the screaming man to his feet.

Sam's hands were empty. He didn't know how or when that had happened, either, but he was so glad it had.

God, I could have killed him. Thank You for keeping me from that.

He looked up, and the room came into focus. The officer still held the cuffs, and Donovan sagged in his grip, with his head bent, quieter now. He was crying, great, heaving sobs shaking his shoulders.

Grams squatted next to Sam. "You OK?"

Sam looked over her shoulder at Robin. Her gaze met his, and Sam closed his eyes. "I will be."

৵৹৶

"I'll bet it feels odd to be in the back of the ambulance instead of driving it." Robin twisted her head on the gurney where they'd strapped her. She and Sam had both protested—she was fine, Donovan hadn't had a chance to hurt her. But the EMT's insisted, and finally Sam had agreed. No one had listened to Robin's opinion. They'd just bundled her up and tied her in place like a baby into a car seat.

Sam shrugged, hard to do as he crouched beside her. "I'm not always driving. I get to ride back here a lot, with patients."

"Oh, right. I forgot." Robin straightened and winced. Parts of her that she didn't remember getting hurt were beginning to complain at every movement. Her neck ached. Her shoulder and elbow burned, along with a few places on her face. She closed her eyes and an image of landing on the beads as she hit the floor caused her to snap them open again. Funny how she could remember something so vividly when she hadn't paid attention to it while it happened.

"It's going to take me years to get those beads back up."

"I'll help." Sam shifted and looked at her, trying to smile. His eyes remained troubled.

Robin reached for his hand. "It's over, Sam. They know now that it was Donovan all along, and he's not going to hurt anyone else. You saved the kids. You saved *Kerry*. Everything's fine."

He nodded. Didn't answer.

She said, "Sam?"

He shook his head. "Here I was thinking because I'd found the kids, everything was over. You were home, safe, and no one could hurt you. Instead, no one was protecting you."

Her heart melted, right along with her knees. Good thing they had her strapped to a gurney. She'd have a hard time falling off that. "Yeah. Someone was protecting me. He always takes care of me, just like a good Father does. I'm fine, Sam."

He chuckled, and some of the tension drained from his forehead and eyes. "OK, yeah, God had your back. I'm glad." His hand traced a line down her cheek and ended cupping her chin. "You did good tonight, babe. You took him on and you won. You didn't let him hurt you."

"That was God and me, you meant, right?"

"Of course." His chuckle made her heart sing, now. Sam was sure giving it a workout tonight.

"But you're still awesome." She grinned, though it hurt most of her face. "Kerry's right."

Sam turned away. "I'm not. There were three officers there, in the house. If I hadn't taken him down, one of them would have." He shrugged. "They were ready to cuff him as it was."

"Yeah, they would have done it if they had to. But *you* were the one who did it. You and God, Sam, and God and me."

He looked up from under his lashes. "You're preachin' to the choir, babe."

"As long as the choir's listening."

"I am." He leaned forward and grasped her hand, pulled it closer to him, until his lips could brush the back. His touch sent delicious shivers through Robin, and they served to soften some of the shock. With Sam only inches in front of her face, she could see the fine sprinkling of freckles on his cheeks, and the starlight serrations of color in his eyes.

"When the kids told me he was going after you, I thought my world ended. Robin, I can't live without you." His lashes slipped shut, and he leaned even closer.

His lips on her mouth were soft, light as a question, sparking with electricity. She put her hand on his neck as he deepened the kiss and only when they rounded a corner and he lost his balance did he give her a chance to breathe. "I love you, Robin. And I don't ever want to be in a position where I can't protect you. Even if you don't always need me."

"Oh, I need you." She traced his lips and jaw, the side of his nose, his eyebrows. "Because I love you right back."

"That's good. 'Cuz, things are gonna change around here. I'm going to be a permanent part of your life."

She giggled. "Like you haven't been?"

"Well, yeah, I have." A half smile charmed her. "But now I get a new role."

"Suits me. Suits me just fine." She lifted her chin, angling her mouth closer to his. "I get the feeling they're going to separate us once we get to the hospital, so you'd better kiss me good, now."

෴

Hours later, Robin nestled in Sam's arms. He had lifted her down from the hospital bed in the exam room of the tiny emergency section, and carried her to Kerry's room. Now, he sat with her on his lap. Neither she nor Kerry were going to be walking anywhere on their own for a while, until his leg brace and her crutch were replaced. The hospital rep hadn't held out much hope for a lot of speed, either. He had given them both standard issue tools, but they weren't as useful as ones specially made for them.

"You saved us. And Jake. Man, he was cool! I wish he could come here, but the nurse said they put one of those needles in him so he can't go nowhere. What's that needle called?"

"An IV. It's because Donovan didn't take care of them. He and Becca both need to stay in the hospital for a while."

"I'm glad Jake's mom came to talk to us. She said you're a hero, Sam." He snuggled deeper into the pillows. "I'm glad you're a hero."

Robin tipped her head to brush a kiss against his rough jaw. "Me, too."

Sam looked down, his eyes glinting.

Kerry got his elbow under him and pushed up, so he could talk more easily. "See? Even Robin says it. You're a hero, Sam. You saved everybody's life. I bet they make a statue of you. Hey, they could put it at the baseball field. We could climb on it after the game."

Sam chuckled and bent close to Robin's ear. "I hope he forgets that one pretty quick."

Kerry chattered on. "I didn't know Donovan was the bad guy. You guys knew, but you forgot to tell me, right? Or wait. Robin said you were scared that he'd hurt me if you did. I forgot, Robin. Hey, Sam, for a long time Mama and Dad were afraid it was you, and I was real scared."

Sam sighed, though not loudly, and turned his attention once more back to Kerry. "We thought he might be, but the police didn't believe us."

"But you showed 'em. You saved us. Now you're a hero, and they shouldn't never put heroes in jail, ever, should they?"

"Not Sam, anyway." Robin straightened. "Here's your mom and dad, Kerry. I bet they've got you all checked out, and they can take you home now."

"Good. I'm tired." Kerry's yawn took up more than half his face. "Hey, Daddy, Sam's a hero. Did you know that, Mom? Sam's a hero."

"I think everybody in the hospital knows." Mr. Wright reached to take Sam's hand.

Sam didn't stand up, but he loosed one hand that was gripped around Robin, to return the shake. "You *are* a hero, Sam. I will never be able to thank you enough for saving my son."

"See? He's a real hero." Fatigue slurred Kerry's words.

"Wasn't me," Sam protested. "It was Jake. He's the one you need to thank."

"Oh, I plan to. But for now, I need to get my family home. I'll carry you to the waiting room, son, but your sister is there with your wheelchair." Mr. Wright turned to Robin. "Do you need one? We have an extra."

"I've got one at home, thanks. Sam'll take care of me."

"Hey." Kerry went from half asleep to wide awake, and he giggled. "You and Sam are getting married, aren't you? 'Cuz you keep kissing when you think my eyes are closed."

"Kerry!" But even his mother laughed.

"You got that right, my friend." Sam wrapped both arms tight around Robin. "Babe, I haven't had time to get a ring. Maybe we can do it together, OK?"

She twisted to stare into his face. "Are you asking me what I think you're asking me?"

"Do I need to? Kerry already told everyone we're getting married." Sam bent and met her lips, and on a sigh, he said, "I will thank God for your life every minute of our marriage, Robin. I don't ever want to come close to losing you again."

Robin didn't notice the Wrights leave. A long time later, still waiting for the nurse to bring her release papers and in no hurry for the woman to come, she patted Sam's chest. "You're my hero, too."

Epilogue

The ring bearer was a bit taller than the typical four-year-old. He walked with a distinct list, and instead of on a pillow, he carried the rings in his uniform cap. To Robin, he was the handsomest, most endearing ring bearer in existence. Not quite as handsome as Sam, but he didn't have to be. Kerry, as Kerry, was perfect, and now, she could use the word without wincing.

She glanced at her husband-to-be, and saw him swipe at a tear. That was enough to get her started. Grace, her matron of honor, handed her a tissue and took her bouquet. That left one hand free to clasp Sam's.

Who cared if the wedding couple wasn't supposed to hold hands during the ceremony? Ever since that night, she'd held on to Sam every chance she got, and she wasn't going to let some wedding planner make her stop now.

Especially since Sam wouldn't let her stop.

The priest said the words uniting them forever, and Sam came in for the kiss, to cheers and clapping. As he lifted his head, he started to laugh and so did Robin. Because Kerry was the loudest in the church.

"Hey, Sam! Hey, Robin. You guys are awesome!"

Thank you for purchasing this Harbourlight title. For other inspirational stories, please visit our on-line bookstore at www.pelicanbookgroup.com.

For questions or more information, contact us at customer@pelicanbookgroup.com.

Harbourlight Books
The Beacon in Christian Fiction™
an imprint of Pelican Ventures Book Group
www.pelicanbookgroup.com

Connect with Us
www.facebook.com/Pelicanbookgroup
www.twitter.com/pelicanbookgrp

To receive news and specials, subscribe to our bulletin
http://pelink.us/bulletin

May God's glory shine through
this inspirational work of fiction.

AMDG

www.ingramcontent.com/pod-product-compliance
Lightning Source LLC
Chambersburg PA
CBHW052045240626
47153CB00006B/2221